Tess felt pretty good about her week's work and sat on the back porch, watching the sun go down. Looking over to the sheriff's house, she saw he was striped to the waist, washing his underarms then his torso. She was mesmerized by the long strokes he made over his tan skin, the muscles bunching and stretching as he washed then rinsed each portion of his body.

She realized she was staring when he went to push down his trousers to bare the rest of his body for ablutions. Lowering her gaze, she moved quickly into her darkened kitchen, making her way upstairs feeling the heat of a blush on her face.

She chided herself for her foolishness. She had seen naked men as cadavers, during surgeries and examinations, at much closer quarters. Why should this man be so much more interesting to her? He was attractive and an excellent specimen of manhood, but would that make her heart beat faster merely thinking of him becoming naked in front of her?

Forever Kind of Woman

by

Susan Payne

Forever Kind of Woman

The Wild Rose Press, Inc.
PO Box 708
Adams Basin, NY 14410-0708
Visit us at www.thewildrosepress.com

Publishing History
First Edition, 2020
Trade Paperback ISBN 978-1-5092-3242-0
Digital ISBN 978-1-5092-3243-7

Published in the United States of America

Dedication

To my lovely daughters for the hours of reading and encouragement with which they always supported me.

Other Stories by Susan Payne

1886 Rural Texas

CHAPTER ONE

"Forever!" the coach driver yelled out the next stop's name to warn the passengers to get ready to disembark.

Tess bounced on the coach's hard seat, managing a tight smile for the man seated next to her as he bumped into her yet again, knocking her into the wall of the coach on her other side. He was wearing what would pass as cowhand essentials with a careless disregard for personal hygiene. To his credit, he braced his boots against the seat across from them. His spurs tinkled musically with each bump and rut the coach hit.

The two men opposite her did not seem to have as much of a problem with staying within their allotted space. One of the suited men was of indeterminate age. His gray beard gave him the appearance of an old man although his hands, which he'd been using to tip the brown bottle of medicinal tonic to his lips with, appeared much younger. His breath, traveling the short distance to Tess's nostrils, smelled of the ninety proof it surely was.

The second suited man boasting a Derby was a traveling salesman according to the card he passed out to his fellow passengers. He was the most loquacious of them all when the trip began, but after a couple of days, even he had run out of stories to tell or things to remark upon.

During this last grueling portion of the trip, Tess had had plenty of time to rethink her hastily made plans to travel all the way to Texas in response to a few letters written between herself and the bachelor doctor who lived in the town. She hoped he was as nice as he seemed in their correspondence, that he was as caring as he sounded when writing of the town's need for medical attention. He'd written that he needed the help of both a trained nurse as well as a wife.

Forever. The town had been Tess's destination for the last four days, maybe for her entire life. She patted her hair to make sure it was still entwined tightly in the proper bun at the back of her head and the dyed straw poke bonnet tied securely below her chin.

The dust, which had found its way through the coach's floorboards, lay in every crease of her black mourning dress, the only good dress she owned. She could not do anything at this point to make her less than pristine appearance any more acceptable. She still wished she could make a good impression upon finally meeting her fiancé.

Tess had sent a tintype of herself with her first letter to her soon-to-be-husband and he hadn't stopped writing after receiving it. After several months of correspondence with the doctor in Forever, Tess was almost there, finally, to become his wife.

Just as she had been once before, well, maybe not actually the same, since this time her new husband wanted the marriage to be complete. The doctor wrote he was looking forward to starting a family as well as gaining a helpmate with his medical work.

The stagecoach came to a rocking stop as a thin young man came out of the stage's ticket office and pulled the door open with a flourish. "Welcome, folks. Last stop for this stage. Tickets for your return trip can be purchased through that door."

Must be not many came to stay in Forever, despite the name. Tess smiled at the fresh-faced young man wearing a poorly-ironed white shirt and pants held up by suspenders to his thin frame. He evidently took his job for the Weber & Weber Coach Line very seriously, as he carefully supervised the unloading of the crates and luggage.

The guard tossed down the luggage tied to the top of the coach.

"Oh, please be careful of that small trunk, it contains very valuable and fragile items," Tess said.

"You shouldn't let people know you have valuables, ma'am," said a soft-spoken male voice behind her. "It makes you a target for thieves and burglars."

Tess turned, excited to see the man she came to marry, but stopped the wide smile that would have changed the appearance of her entire face. Not letting her disappointment show she replied, "Thank you for your concern, Sheriff, but the items are valuable because they are difficult to replace. The value is to me only, since they belonged to my father."

She noted from a medical perspective, he was very well formed, a man who worked for a living. His tan, cotton cavalry shirt with the button-fall was pulled taught over a well-muscled chest. The darker tan trousers, held on to slim hips with a wide belt and shiny military buckle, was prominently displayed over a manly bulge. His worn boots were without spurs, and the gun and holster tied to his thigh spoke of a man who meant business.

His velvet voice of reason brought her eyes back up to his face. "Well, now, ma'am, that ain't written on the trunk, now is it? Just a warning. This isn't a city like you may be used to. There are men here who won't think twice about robbing a little thing like you."

"Isn't that why the town has a sheriff?" Tess asked as she gazed into the gray eyes of the man, a little surprised to find a smile on his stubble covered face.

"I suppose you're right ma'am. My mistake. May I help you take those cases over to the boarding house? Although I have to tell you Mrs. White doesn't usually rent rooms to women, just on-the-road salesmen mostly."

Looking around the now dusty, empty street, Tess stammered, "I, I guess lodging wasn't discussed with, Doctor Waverly. He should be here since I sent a wire letting him know when I was arriving."

"You here to meet with the doctor?" the sheriff asked. He shouted to the boy in the ticket office, "Hey, Abe, you got a wire for the doctor?"

"Yep, came on this coach, Abe shouted back. "I'll take it over as soon as I get these boxes locked away."

Disappointed, Tess grimaced. "I guess I should have asked a few more questions before I bothered to send that wire. Is Doctor Waverly's office close-by? He said it was right on the main street." She perused the few short blocks of town, squinting in the midday sun.

"Not too far. Let me get those bags." Scooping up the trunk after piling Tess's few other possessions on top and moved off. "If you'll just follow me, I can show you where it is."

She tried to keep up with his long strides, carrying the black bag that was never far from her. He stopped in front of a white, two-story clapboard house with a wide front porch. From the porch roof hung a sign reading, Doctor Waverly, General Practice.

The sheriff took the two steps up to the house's porch. He looked at a note tucked onto a nail and turned to Tess saying, "The doctor's out at the Major's place, about an hour and a half east of here. I can maybe send someone out there, but it will be a day or so until he gets back to town. The Major's been a patient for years. Bad ticker."

"No, I don't want the doctor to think he needs to come back, especially leaving a patient who may be in need of him. I, umm, I can just stay here until the doctor returns," Tess decided aloud.

The sheriff hesitated then asked, "You and the doctor have some kind of arrangement?"

Tess, angry the sheriff was questioning her integrity and honor, said forcefully, "I am here at Doctor Waverly's invitation to become his wife."

The sheriff squinted at her, seemingly to find any reason the doctor would have done something that dumb. Tess tried not to stomp her foot in frustration.

He finally said, "The doors unlocked. If you need anything I live behind the jail, right next door."

Now Tess really could use a good foot stomping, since this bear of a man was to be her neighbor, and he seemed to find her wanting for brains and looks.

"I will be fine. Doctor Waverly will be back sooner or later."

"By the way, the name's Noah, or if you'd rather, Sheriff Carter, at your service." The grin that brought out the hidden dimples had returned to his tanned face. Tess suspected he was enjoying her discomposure.

Not to seem rude, Tess smiled. "I'm, Mrs. Tess McLeish." As the sheriff's eyebrows rose, she added, "My late husband was Doctor Torrey McLeish of Chicago." As far as an explanation went, it wasn't much. No one here would have heard of the renowned surgeon or his young wife and their research into the latest medical procedures.

"Ma'am," the sheriff said touching the brim of his hat. He descended the porch steps and headed toward the boardwalk in front of the jail.

Tess tried the doorknob which turned easily in her hand. Holding her black bag, she went in to peruse her new home-to-be. A set of polished stairs led up to the sleeping rooms which she thought she'd ignore until later. She would not want her future husband to think she was snooping. The pleasant parlor area immediately off the entry was charming and held an ornately designed nickel-plated stove in one corner. With its finial, it stood taller than her. A sofa and matching chairs with footrests held center stage on a print carpet. Two tables holding clear glass oil-lamps finished the conversation area. An alcove held a roll-top desk and green-glass lamp.

She continued looking on the main floor. After all, it could be quite a while before Doctor Waverly returned home. Getting acquainted with the house she would be in charge of didn't seem inappropriate in the slightest.

All the walls seemed to be of painted plaster with natural woodwork, the floors stained a dark brown, almost as deep as coffee. The parlor led to a dining room, where the table had been pushed to one side and the chairs set around the perimeter. Evidently the area used by waiting patients. An alcove with pocket doors that slid into the wall served as an examination room. To the side was a small room with space enough for two cots and a wheeled chair between them.

The examination room was the most interesting for Tess. The one high, covered window allowed light into the white paneled room. In the center was an examination table, a wheeled stool and a movable table on small enameled wheels. The tall glassed-door case boasted several shelves filled with brown, green, and clear glass bottles and jars. Tess read their labels. They held exotic herbs and medicines, many of which Tess knew. She had even more in the trunk of which she was so protective.

Tess did not open the drawers in the cabinet's lower portion. She knew they would hold the tools of the trade, tools which she did not want to contaminate. The examination room was well-organized and clean, but then Tess realized the whole house had been that way so far.

She moved into the kitchen finding that room as clean and neat as the rest of the house. The handpump was next to a sink on a wooden frame. A bright yellow gingham cloth had been tacked onto the framework to hide the pipes. A natural wood cabinet with a flour box and sifter built into it stood next in line. The cabinet with an enameled pullout shelf also held other food items and spices that showed through the glass paned doors. Another cabinet on the end wall held the china and baking dishes.

A rectangular table with four chairs stood in place-of-honor under a window with more yellow gingham curtains hanging from it. Glancing through the glass, she saw the bare dirt back yard. The floor, covered with linoleum, bore a colorful rag rug near the rear door that led onto a laundry porch, the upper sections of which were left open to the weather.

A plate and cup in the sink, ready for washing, made Tess think Doctor Waverly had left in a hurry, so his trip was not planned. If the Major was elderly, Doctor Waverly might have left as soon as a summons arrived.

After getting the wood stove lit, Tess filled the water kettle. She returned to the porch to retrieve the rest of her luggage. She considered whether she should lock the front door to protect herself and her belongings. Then decided if Doctor Waverly left his door open, crime wasn't as rampant as the sheriff had tried to insinuate.

Once those items were in the foyer, Tess removed her hat and went in search of tea, hoping it would not be a lost cause. She found what she was looking for in the flour cabinet, along with white sugar. A bonanza for a woman who had been travelling by stage. Days of facing meals consisting of unsavory meat stew and a stale roll. And something that passed for coffee but tasted much like the dishwater she hoped the dishes had been cleaned in.

This was not the welcome she envisioned when she first set out for Forever. She had

expected to be met by the kind, considerate fiancé she learned to know through their correspondence. They would walk to the church for a quiet wedding service and then on to their home. Thoughts of the evening activity following would have to wait. She had neither the experience or imagination to think further not having had any practical knowledge of the physical joining of a man and woman. Her marriage with Doctor McLeish had been one of convenience and not a love match.

Tess sat at the kitchen table, contemplating her new life and looking out at the yard. What grass there was appeared dead but was surrounded with bushes budding with potential flowers. A movement out of the side of her eye caught her attention. The sheriff stepped onto the back porch and rapped on the door, making its small window rattle.

Tess rose and opened the door. "May I help you, Sheriff?" she asked as if she were already the lady of the house.

"I wanted to make sure you were comfortable and there was food for you until the doctor gets back." He looked about the kitchen. His gaze stopped at her cup and saucer on the table. "I see you've settled in."

"I'm used to settling in quickly. I accompanied my late husband on calls, and often fixed meals for an entire family if the mother was ill or in childbed. I had my own patients, too, whom I cared for."

"So, you're a regular doctor? Not a veterinarian?" At the shake of her head, he continued, "Too bad, we need one. Folks will pay a lot more to heal a sick cow than they will to set a cowhand's broken ankle."

"Do you think that is where my…." She stumbled and finished, "Doctor Waverly is? Working on cattle?" Tess wondered if animal care was going to become part of her practice. It wasn't something she had planned on doing.

"Never known him to do so before. If he's out to the Major's he's probably dealing with a health issue. Like I said, the Major is gettin' on in age and has been dealing with this heart condition for years. His daughter even came to say good-bye. She lives with her mother back east and has done so for year."

Tess nodded taking in this new information. "It's good to know Doctor Waverly cares so much for his patients. A doctor in this kind of town needs to be part of the family. People depend on him for more than their health care. A good doctor cares for their entire mental and physical well-being. There are studies out encouraging medical professionals to counsel their patients in eating habits and adding calisthenics or walking into their daily routine."

"I doubt a farmer needs to do more walking," he said derisively.

"No, not men and women who do manual labor, but many ladies and some gentlemen no longer do physical work. They sit behind office desks or have a woman-of-all-work come in daily to care for their home and children. It makes them lazy and those patients tend to have health problems directly related to sloth and gluttony, two of the seven sins," she stated primly.

He scoffed. "Now you're sounding too much like Reverend Jenkins and I get enough of that on Sunday morning." Walking away, he added, "If you need anything today, I'm usually right next door."

CHAPTER TWO

Carter, his chair tipped back against the office wall, nodded off in the heat of the quiet day. His hat slanted over his eyes, he had just about reached that pleasant place of balance between sleep and wakefulness.

He jumped when he heard a horse galloping into town, then pull to a stop nearby. He reached the door in time to see a young cowhand jump onto the porch next door and beat on the wood and glass doorframe, yelling for the doctor.

Knowing the doctor wasn't there, he called out, "What's the commotion about, son? Why do you need the doctor so badly?"

"Jake, he got gored by a bull and it near took his leg off," the young man told the sheriff excitedly. "I wuz sent to git the doctor before he bleeds to death. That's what the boss said to tell the doc anyway. He didn't look good to me."

"Doctor Waverly ain't here, he's another forty miles out of town, and I don't know when he'll be back for sure. I suppose you can ride on out to the Major's spread and see if he will come back with you."

The youth looked crestfallen.

Tess appeared at the door and spoke up, "I can go back with you as soon as I get my bag and case. If it's as bad as you say, the injured man won't be alive by the time you get Doctor Waverly."

The young man looked gratefully at the woman then his expression became doubtful. "I don't know, ma'am. I mean, the boss said to git Doc Waverly."

The sheriff took one look at Tess's stubborn face and said, "That's alright, son. Ride back and tell Wilson I'm bringing Doctor McLeish out with me. I'll take any heat from your boss if he cares to pass some on."

"I can get a buggy and go on my own if someone can direct me," Tess told them both. "The livery does rent buggies, doesn't it?"

"Yeah, and I'll go get it. Doc, you go and get the things you think you may need." He spun on one boot and headed to the livery at the other end of Main Street.

The young man, still standing next to his horse jumped as the sheriff yelled over his shoulder, "Go on back to the ranch, son, and tell them we're on the way. Don't waste time arguing."

Tess was ready and dressed with a grey cape over her dull brown dress. A dyed straw bonnet without frills set on top of her unflattering hairstyle. She held her black bag, but pointed to the small trunk. "Sheriff, if you can find a place for that in the buggy, I'd appreciate it." He got down from the seat, his long stride eating up the distance. He placed the heavy case into the seat alcove on the back of the buggy, thinking the woman should learn to pack lighter. "You really need all this stuff?"

"It holds my saws and cutting tools. I may need to remove a leg and I'll need the bigger tools to do a proper job of it," she answered bluntly as she settled her skirts around her feet in the confined area of the buggy.

Carter grunted in approval. Evidently, this was a sensible woman without all that fake faint-of-heart bullshit. He whipped up the horse to get them on their way.

Handling the reins easily he felt he had to say something before reaching the ranch. "Ma'am, this ain't gonna be like a big city. When things like this happen, the man gets fixed up as best as he can be. Cowboys know the dangers from the start. No one will think less of you if you find you can't handle the job."

"I will think less of me, Sheriff. I am trained as a surgeon. It has been my misfortune to have assisted at more amputations than I would care to remember. Although we have come a long way since the war, it is still a trying event for all involved."

The ride remained silent, each passenger evidently thinking about what was to come, and how they planned to handle it.

As Carter pulled into the ranch gates, he saw a group of men crowded around the bunkhouse door. Driving the buggy over to the side, he got out to help Tess dismount, only to find her already striding toward the group of men. They parted like the Red Sea must have so long ago. There were some mumblings from the group, but no one challenged her right to be there or to get to the injured man. The young cowhand must have done some quick explaining because the boss approached the sheriff first, ignoring Tess completely.

Wilson warned sounding frustrated, "Carter, you better know what you're doing." The rancher glanced at the petit woman continuing, "I know Doc Waverly ain't close enough to fetch in time, but Jake's wound looks bad. He needs a doctor, not a soft word and handholding. That can come afterwards."

Tess answered for herself directly to the rancher. "I can see by the leg's position it's a compound fracture. The man may lose his leg if the bone is crushed. I know what has to be done and can do it, sir."

Hearing no further protests, she turned toward the others. "Now I will need most of you to clear out and give me some room. Sheriff, if you would pull his boots and cut his trousers off, I can examine the wound and see where we go from there."

Tess washed her hands and shouted over her shoulder in a tone that brooked no argument. "I'll need more clean water from a pail not used as a slop bucket." Tying on a clean apron from her black bag, she turned back to her patient covered his private parts with the towel she brought over for that purpose.

Smelling her patient's breath to be sure, she said, "So you have anesthetized the patient prior to surgery? Thank you, it makes shorter work than having to do so myself, although alcohol thins the blood and makes it flow freer. It was still the right thing to do in this case."

She felt along his leg, one hand on the inside starting at his crotch, the other on the outside pressing in to feel how the bones were placed. Her mind pictured the man's skeleton. How each bone fit to the next. How the tendons and muscles held them together. She continued her exploration to his knee.

"The leg bone is broken a few inches below the hip. Although he's lost a lot of blood, it appears the wound can be staunched without cauterizing it. He's going to end up with quite a scar to brag about."

Wilson and two other men who'd stayed to watch let out deep sighs of relief. Even if they didn't trust her abilities yet, she assumed, they still believed her prognosis.

"All right, Sheriff, if you would hold on to the patient as much as you're able, I can do the rest." At Carter's surprise, she continued, "Grab him under the arms and hold tight. Don't let him slide toward me. I need to set the bone and it's been pulled out of place by the tendons. Got him?"

The sheriff nodded to let her know he was ready.

Tess walked to the end of the table, placed her foot up between the injured man's legs, and pulled with all her strength on the broken leg. Pushing off from the table, she used her full length to stretch the tendons. A loud, long moan of pain came from the insentient patient in response before falling unconscious again.

Tess twisted the foot then yanked until a slight grinding of bone on bone could be heard and a final popping sound. Her lips turned up into a smile as she held the leg in place.

Ignoring the stare Wilson and the other two men gave her skirt which had slid downward from her raised leg, exposing some ankle, she strained to keep the bone from pulling apart again. She continued to hold Jake's leg in place, to teach the tendons where they belonged once more.

"Eyes right!" barked the sheriff. Every man's head swiveled to the right to stare at the angry man at the head of the table.

Tess ignored the men realizing the sheriff was concerned for her modesty and thought what a nice man he is. I really should be more grateful for his help.

Tess pulled her foot from the man's crotch, stepped to the side of her patient, and again pressed her small hands down the leg assessing the alignment. Satisfied with her work, she sighed.

"That's the leg. I was afraid I would need to cut it open to set the bone, but it was a clean break and snapped back together. Now I'll strap-it and take care of the wound where the bull's horn did so much damage."

Tess wanted to finish before the cowhand woke. Getting the job finished correctly her only concern at the time. Using her usual neat stitches, she sutured both wounds, then covered them with clean gauze bandages.

The patient moaned only half-conscious but the pain was rousing him. He began twisting his body trying to escape the agony, but a gentle hand on his shoulder kept him at ease.

"Who will be in charge of his care?"

A scruffy looking cowhand with gray frizzled beard steeped forward. "That'd be me, ma'am. Name's Stubby cuz of 'an unfortunate mishap' while brandin' cattle and the rope cuttin' off two of my fingers." He held up his left hand missing the two first digits.

"I hate to get a patient too dependent on laudanum. It can become more of a problem than the pain." She showed him the small glass bottle of cloudy liquid. "There's enough here to keep him comfortable for the next two days. He can have only broth for the next week since he must stay quiet and use a bedpan. He'll need to stay off his feet for at least six-weeks to make sure it's healed. No hopping to the privy no matter what for at least a month. That would knock everything out of place again."

Stubby shook his head sadly. "Don't know how to cook no broth. What is it?"

"Take a soup pot half-filled with water and place a joint of meat in it, preferably from the bull that gored him." Stubby stifled a chuckle as Tess continued, "And boil it with a little salt, pepper and a lot of onion. When the meat is falling off the bone, it's ready to eat, but only give him the broth. When it cools and forms gelatin, serve him that, too. He needs good nourishment to rebuild that bone and make more blood."

Tess made sure the older man understood all her instructions about changing the bandages and signs to look for in case of an infection.

She washed up and put her tools away after supervising the removal of the patient from the hard table to the almost as hard mattress on his cot. She told Stubby to send for her if the man developed a fever or if the wounded areas got red or swollen.

"I'll be back out in a couple of days unless my, I mean, Doctor Waverly returns. In that case, I'll turn the patient over to him."

Mr. Wilson stepped closer to her. "Thank-you, ma'am. We really appreciate your comin' way out here. The sheriff said he's to see you home. I'm a believer now, so if we need a doctor, either one of you should feel free to come."

Tess appreciated the praise. She had been leery after the reception she had gotten. Hadn't realized how rare a female practitioner was here in the west. She would need to reassess her future dealing with the citizens of the area. At least the males. Hopefully the females were more accepting.

Tess relaxed feeling vindicated. Sheriff Carter standing up for her, even when he wasn't sure of her abilities, touched her deeply. Usually men needed to be shown what she could do before they took her seriously. Carter had done so because he believed in her, that she would not claim to be able to do something she couldn't.

After taking care of necessities in the surprisingly clean privy, Tess was surprised to see it had turned dark while she'd been busy in the bunkhouse with her patient. There had been several lamps inside, and now it seemed pitch black. She could see neither barn nor corral nor ranch house.

The sheriff met her. "You'll get used to it in a moment. There's enough moonlight to get back to town if we take it easy. I told Wilson I didn't want to take the time to sit down to a meal so the missus sent some food home with us. I hope that was alright with you." He handed her up into the buggy making sure her skirt was tucked into the buggy and wouldn't get tangled in the wheel

"That's fine. I was so deep in thought coming out here I didn't pay attention to how far it was or how long it took. I hate even to contemplate removing a limb from a healthy man. It changes their life so completely and often becomes a stigma that's difficult to live through, hence Stubby's name."

"That's the only name I know him by, Doc." Carter said as he concentrated on keeping the horse on the road. "It happened when he was just starting out and he uses his lost fingers to remind the young cowhands how easy it is to lose something vital when you let your mind wander. I'm sure he's gonna use this poor cowhand's injuries as an example to others. Not only to tease him for sleeping through the whole part of a pretty, young woman placing her hands all over his nether regions."

Tess took a deep breath. "I most certainly did not touch his…his nether regions. Not even near," she said while knowing it was a lie. Although she had tried not to notice when she touched him near his nether regions, which to her was much the same thing.

"As you say, Doc. Why don't you look in that flour bag and see what they sent us home with? I can't believe you're not starving, too, after all that pulling and twistin'." There was good humor in his voice. "I know it's hard cider in the jug. Just pull the cork and hand it to me if you will."

The cider took precedence as she handed it to him so that he drank from the spout one handed while the crock rested against his elbow. Tess took note of the proper etiquette of drinking while riding planning on copying it when the jug was returned to her.

Tess unwrapped the sandwiches and inspected them by moonlight. "Looks like ham, and there are apples and some kind of spice cake squares. I can smell ginger and cinnamon." She handed half to Carter, then a second when that disappeared quickly.

They travelled along the road eating the divided food and taking pulls from the jug of cider. Tess noticed that once away from the ranch, the moon did appear brighter and the road showed easily between the bushes and trees lining the way. Just as she felt her head begin to nod, Tess was brought back to reality with a start.

"Damnation!" hollered Carter. Then a softer, "Whoa, boy, whoa."

Tess heard Carter try to calm the horse now harnessed to a tipsy buggy. She knew one of the wheels had snapped off its axil as it fell into a rut near the edge of the road.

Tess reached out her hand. "I'll hold the reins while you get the horse unharnessed. Is he hurt?"

Carter walked to the head of the horse stroking the animal's back the entire way. His soothing tone calming yet firm, letting the animal know that the man was in charge and the man would get things straightened out. Soon his hand reached up to take the reins from Tess.

"He's fine. I'm going to tie him over here out of the way, then see what we've got to work with."

A short time later, he climbed back onto the seat sending the buggy rocking. "Well, this is as far as we can go tonight, Doc. Don't happen to have any blankets in that case, do you?"

"No, but there is the one we've been sitting on. Better over us than under us at this point. It's a lap robe so it should be fairly warm." She pulled the blanket out from under them and placed it over both of their laps.

"Doc, I don't need the blanket." Pushing the blanket back toward her.

"Oh, yes you do, because I plan on using your warmth. The least I can do is help you hold your body heat in for both of us." She removed her bonnet and turned her back to him.

There was laughter in the sheriff's voice as he answered meekly, "Yes, sir, I mean Ma'am." He turned in his seat to face her, then drew her gently to himself. Settling into the buggy seat, he stretched out to the farthest corner he could while Tess curled into his side, holding the blanket corner up to her chin.

Finally, they were both comfortable, well, as comfortable as two people can be sitting in the chilly night air in a buggy with a slight lean to it. The silence was unusual because Tess was used to city life. Since leaving Chicago, there had been much less nightly noise but she found the chirps and clicks of night creatures reassuring. That there was life all around her.

Tess became curious about her new neighbor and turned in his arms to look up at him. "Carter, do you have a military background? Seems to me you are used to giving orders and expecting them to be followed."

"Well, I was in the Army for a number of years. I planned on making it a career and reached the rank of Lieutenant Colonel, but then lost my taste for the whole thing. I like being a lawman, though. I think I'm pretty good at it, although it's kind of quiet around Forever." He paused, wishing he had brought his tobacco. He liked a smoke at night to get him ready to sleep, to relax and he certainly needed something to relax him with this female snuggling closer and closer to him every time she wiggled.

"So, why'd you leave? The Army, I mean. There seems to be a lot of forts and they all require officers as well as troops."

"They do, and I was one. A fort officer, that is, at one time. But..." He hesitated telling this woman the truth for some reason, not that he had ever told anyone else either. "I guess I got tired of the killing of the tribes. I mean, we bested them. They were desperate, tired people trying to keep some semblance of their civilization and we just kept gnawing away at any little bit that was left. Emasculating their men." When he felt her tense, he said hastily, "Not physically, more mentally, I guess. We made them less than men, then jeered at their impotency. I didn't want to be part of it any more. We watched as women and children starved on the reservations, we forced them to move onto, then arrested and hanged the braves for going out and hunting for food for their families."

He stopped and thought back to how he felt as a younger man, facing the reality that life was flawed and his beliefs challenged. "A man has to stand up for what he believes is right. I did, then resigned my commission."

With a much lighter tone, he continued, "I rode around for a while enjoying the freedom to do as I wished without asking permission or taking orders. I found Forever one day and stayed when the town-founders asked me to be their sheriff."

"I didn't realize the U.S. Government was being so abhorrent to the Indians," she said quietly. "No wonder some of them leave the reservations and try to live free, as they have always done. One could almost understand their need for retaliation, take back their lands, even by killing those they blame their loss on."

"That's where it gets tricky. Is it retribution for past sins or a punishment for disobeying a federal law? I understood the need to go out after raiding parties, but at the same time, we were breaking every promise we ever made the Chiefs. I found no way to live with the consequences."

"I'm glad you found Forever. You seem to be a part of the town. That must be a good feeling, like coming home," she said drowsily, sounding as if she were unable to stay awake.

Carter was getting tired too because he stopped talking and listened to her even breathing as he fell asleep.

"Whoa, hey folks, you need some help?" The shout woke Carter from a sound sleep. He opened his eyes to see the foreman of the Rocking R sitting high in his wagon peering doubtfully at the couple bundled up to their noses in a blanket.

Carter pushed down the blanket and tried to sit up when he became very aware of the young woman in his lap. Tess, her hair a mess from rubbing into his chest, was slow to stir as she sat up beside him and yawned.

"Yeah, I can do with a little help." Carter began explaining, pointing to Tess as he climbed down, "I was driving Dr. McLeish, here, home from fixing a broken leg at the Double J when I let the wheel go into a rut. Didn't see it in the dark. I'd appreciate you driving her into town while I ride the horse back. The livery will have to come out with another wheel or find some way to haul this one back on a wagon."

"Sure, got plenty of room here." He slid to one side of the warn wooden bench. "Where do I drop her off?" the man asked, still speaking to the sheriff as if talking to a woman was anathema to him.

"She's a visitor of Doctor Waverly's. Just set her off there and if you could, take this case with her. She needs it if she gets another call for help."

"Will do, but you're sure you'll be alright?" the man asked shifting his reins to both hands.

"Well, the horse ain't broke for riding, but he'll know what I want him to do by the time I get him back to town," Carter said with a laugh.

The wagon pulled away, leaving Carter to fold up the blanket and place it on the horse, hoping to lessen the animal's discouragement to his being rode. Carter would take this time riding back to town to figure out exactly what he made of his night spent with the affianced doctor. And why she was still on his mind.

CHAPTER THREE

Tess arrived home and thanked the driver she had a nice conversation with even if it took half the trip before he warmed up enough to converse with her. Entering the house, she found it the same as when she ran out the night before, so no Dr. Waverly, yet. She continued through the house and out to the privy to take care of an immediate need.

Re-doing her hair into the proper bun pulled tightly to the back of her head, she washed her face and neck at the kitchen sink. Going to the back porch, she brushed the road dust from her brown dress. It would have to do until she could get a bath and change of clothes. She still felt hesitant to move-in completely until she spoke with Doctor Waverly. Would she always think of him as such? She never called her first husband by his Christian name.

She placed a small roast she found in the cold-box down the well into the oven. She was searching for root vegetables when she heard a noise coming from the front porch. Opening the door, she found an attractive couple standing there, a buggy and horse just outside the porches' steps. The woman wore the most stylish dress Tess had seen west of St. Louis. The waist was tucked-in and the bustle had mounds of fabric draped down like a waterfall to end with several ruffles around the hem to hold the dust down. The woman herself was young and pretty and blond. Large blue eyes fringed by lush lashes blinked quickly as she took in Tess's attire.

The handsome man wore a suit and black tie and sported a Derby.

"May I help you?" asked Tess, thinking the couple was in search of Doctor Waverly.

The young man recovered himself first. "Oh, you must be, Mrs. McLeish? I'm, Doctor Waverly." He stuck out his hand to shake hers.

Tess faltered. How...how embarrassing not to know your own fiancé. "Yes, how do you do?" She hoped she looked more like her photograph than he did his. His had showed a rather morose man with dark sunken eyes and a pouty mouth - not this very attractive man with light brown hair, laughing blue eyes and even dimples. The damn man had dimples.

This was not a man who married dowdy widows. He married blond haired, blue-eyed nymphs like the one standing next to him on the porch. Oh no, the thought chased through her mind, he hadn't run off and married this woman, had he?

"May I introduce Miss Millicent Philips? Millicent is the daughter of Major Phillips whom I've been attending recently. She needed to head east so I said I would gladly drive her back to town with me and take care of her until the stage arrives."

"How thoughtful, of you, doctor," said Tess. She stepped back to welcome the man and his guest into his own home. She wondered if Doctor Waverly had told Millicent what Tess was really doing in his house, or was he trying to keep the fact he was an engaged man to himself. Tess decided to see how things progressed. Possibly the doctor was only interested in helping his patient's daughter return home. Tess didn't want to admit she had seen his admiring gaze land on the beauty several times already.

"I'm so fatigued, Robert, you wouldn't mind if I rest before dinner, would you? I'm not a good traveler, as I explained." She turned to Tess. "I'll set the dress out for you to wipe down." "These back roads are so dusty one can't go anywhere without a completely new ensemble." Then she glided up the stairs with 'Robert' following her, carrying two of the smaller cases.

Tess turned back to the kitchen where she would increase the amount of food she was preparing, knowing Millicent wouldn't eat very much. Too fattening or too common or too tasteless, Tess was sure. Tossing more potatoes into the sink, Tess began to calm down enough to think rationally. It wasn't Millicent's fault Tess felt caught in a less than perfect light. It wasn't as if Tess had any unrealistic expectations or grand idea, she was a temptress in any way. If Doctor Waverly was smitten with the beauty then there was nothing Tess could do. Besides, the woman was going to be leaving and then Tess and the doctor would go on as they had planned. Tess looked down thinking she was being less than charitable when 'Robert' entered the kitchen and apologized.

"I am sorry Millicent took you to be my housekeeper, Mrs. McLeish. I never thought you would be here so soon. Although I did urge you to come as soon as you got everything closed-up in Chicago. I thought you would send a wire." He had managed to turn the apology into a reprimand.

She was not going to let him get away with it. "I did send a telegram. It arrived on the coach with me. You never told me the town doesn't have a telegraph

line and that wire messages come by way of coach."
She wouldn't be cowed by a mere man.

"Yes, sorry, I didn't think everything through it
seems. I have been out taking care of a patient who has
been very good to me since I got here to Forever. That's
why I agreed to aid his daughter in returning to her
home." He turned his nose toward the oven. "My, it
does smell delicious, is there anything I can do to help?
I usually cook for myself, ever since I lost my
housekeeper last summer."

"Just before we began to write to each other, then?
You didn't tell me about her either," Tess began to see
why 'Robert' found himself in need of a wife. It wasn't
only because he wanted a helpmate with his workload
here. In fact, so far, it didn't appear the doctor's office
was very busy at all. If it were, then Robert wouldn't
have been able to go for several days in a row to a
ranch, hours out of town.

"I was very distraught at the time. Everything
seemed to be changing. I found it over-whelming.
When you answered my request for a nurse or doctor
needing a place to start, I was excited that we could
have the same relationship you and your husband once
had. I can't tell you how impressed I am with your
husband's medical pamphlets."

"I published scientific journals, also. My husband
encouraged me to write about the advances we made in
surgery and the use of chloroform. They were well
received." Tess defended her own medical experience
then became angry she felt the need to do so.

"Well, now you won't have to worry about such
things. I can handle most medical conditions, but it
would be nice to have someone to care for the patients

if they need to stay here to recuperate. You've seen the side room, I take it," he asked, showing the most animation since Millicent went upstairs.

"I am used to having more responsibilities, Robert." Deciding to go on as she thought best, she tried to gauge Robert's views of her doing the same here in Forever. "I saw patients, especially pregnant women and the older ladies who felt more comfortable speaking with a female doctor."

She reminded him, "We corresponded about my strong interest in starting a center for women who need to have their breasts removed due to cancer. I still wish to proceed with those plans."

"We'll see. This all may be theoretical, of course. There aren't very many women in town and they seem to handle their own birthing and such. Now I'm going up to change clothes for dinner. Can we eat in the formal dining room and use the good china? That would be so much nicer for Millicent. She's used to living in better conditions then here in Forever." He excused himself and went upstairs he explained to rest, also.

Tess, who spent most of the cold night sleeping upright after spending hours setting a leg and suturing wounds, washed and cut the vegetables. She prepared a butter cream sauce for them as she reminded herself the dinner was for her as much as anyone else.

She did not want to start out with an argument or anger at her fiancé. After all, he hadn't known she would be arriving, so he had not intentionally missed meeting her stage. He seemed to still think of her as remaining with him, in Forever, so possibly she was over-sensitive to his attention to Millicent. After all, he may be as chivalrous with every woman he meets, apparently just not his betrothed.

Robert and Millicent came downstairs together to be met with the dining room chandelier lit, a lace tablecloth and sparkling china, crystal and flatware at each place setting. All four of them.

"Are we having another guest?" Robert asked, admiring the centerpiece of greenery with ribbons and a strand of pearls woven through it.

"Yes, Sheriff Carter is invited since he was so welcoming and was such a help to me yesterday when I was called out to the Double J to set a broken leg."

As Robert pulled out the chair for Millicent, Tess returned to the kitchen to serve up the roast. A rap on the backdoor announced the sheriff's arrival. Carter grabbed a couple of the serving dishes while Tess brought in the roast placing it in front of Robert, who was already seated. Carter set the dishes on the table, then held the chair for Tess. He took his seat opposite her on the side of the table. Robert said a brief grace, then began to carve the roast.

He turned to Sheriff Carter. "It seems I owe you some thanks for taking care of Mrs. McLeish when she arrived. I'm sorry if she was a bother, I would have told her this wasn't a good time for a visit if I had received her wire in time to prevent her arrival."

Tess felt anger rising within her breast. He had spoken as if she were not even in the room. She was about to tear a strip off Robert for his boorish behavior, when Carter turned to her and said, 'This is a truly excellent roast, Doctor McLeish, and the gravy is delicious." He continued to compliment the roast, the gravy, the mashed potatoes, the creamed vegetables and the wonderful smell of the pie cooling in the kitchen.

Tess stared at Carter with her lips pressed together tightly as he smiled. She cooled her anger and decided to follow his lead. She would wait until a better time to ask Robert the all-important question - has he changed his mind?

Millicent ate a few bites of each item then patted her rosebud mouth daintily with the napkin. "I couldn't imagine eating the portion Robert had given me."

Millicent eyed Tess's plate. Tess had been eating as if she intended no food to go to waste. Tess didn't know if the men considered her a pig or not, but she wasn't going to stop eating half-way through her meal.

Tess stood to clear the table and Carter did the same. When they entered the kitchen, Tess pointed towards the sink. "Thank you, Sheriff Carter. Just pile them in there. I'll get to them later."

His eyes twinkled. "I'll help. Kind of like singing for my supper."

"This was supposed to be a thank-you for taking me out to the Double J. I owe you for the buggy rental and the broken wheel." She handed him the dessert plates while she took the pie and server before leading him back to the dining room. They must have interrupted Millicent and Robert because both became quiet and Millicent was rosy with a blush due to something the two were talking about.

Again, Carter helped Tess into her seat and when the dessert was eaten, which Millicent did not turn down although left much of the crust. Carter helped clear the table while Robert took his guest into the parlor to entertain her

In the kitchen, Tess took the boiling water from the stove and poured it into the sink tub to wash the dishes. Carter took a dishtowel and as the dishes drained, dried them and stacked them on the kitchen table.

Carter patted his stomach. "The meal was most excellent, Doctor McLeish. Much better than I would have had. Dinner for me is open a can and heat it if it needs it. I don't do anything fancy, sometimes I cook a joint of meat but then there won't be vegetables. Not even sure if I have vegetables. I know the root cellar is empty of everything besides spider webs," he said, trying to keep Tess entertained and her mind off the two sitting alone in the other room. "Oh, may I come over and collect some? Clean webs can be used to stop bleeding and it looks like they might come in handy here. A lot of bulls around isn't there?" she smiled up at him cheekily.

"So, you're not planning on leaving then? I was worried Robert had ticked you off enough to have you packing up and getting on the same coach as Millicent." He watched a series of emotions flit across her face.

"I haven't made up my mind yet, but I certainly don't wish to travel anywhere with Millicent. She seems to think people are there to do her bidding. What will make me leave is if Robert discovers he has feelings for her. Then I would bow out and let them live their lives."

Carter set down the platter he had been wiping. "Even after you came all this way? You'd just go back?" He hoped she wouldn't leave. Something about the woman made him want to search her out, find out more about her. She intrigued him in some way, maybe a lot of ways.

Tess dunked the last pot into the dishwater. "Millicent doesn't seem to be the Forever kind of woman. This town isn't a place she wants to spend much time in. I'm sure she's missing all the entertainments and shopping that comes with the bigger cities. I believe Robert will start to see reason once she's gone." She turned to him with a smile. He and I made a lot of plans - for our life, our work, our future family. I'm willing to give him some time before I go back to my old life, which, since my husband's death, isn't really an option."

"I hope you're right, Doc. I'd hate to have you leave Forever, but right now I'd like to kick Robert's ass up and down Main Street for making you miserable."

"I am far from miserable, Sheriff. Robert and I will have time to talk after Millicent leaves town."

Carter hung the drying towel on a hook and started for the back door.

"You're leaving?" she asked.

"Yeah, tell them I said good bye, I have work to do, and thank you again for the wonderful meal." He smiled and closed the door after himself.

Tess walked into the parlor to find the couple looking through the stereoscope. Millicent was smiling at the antics of the moving picture as she tilted the device back and forth.

Getting their attention, Tess said, "The sheriff said he must leave to catch-up on paper work. I find I'm a little tired, so I'm going to have an early night." The two did not respond. She may as well have been talking to the walls.

Tess went up the stairs, wondering if she had made a mistake jumping at the invitation to come to Forever and become Robert's wife. She should have asked more questions. She should have wondered why a young doctor wanted to marry a widow he had never met.

Tess thought she had grown to know this man as they wrote to one another, but now she had questions. She walked past the pretty guest room Tess decided not to use since she would be moving into the master bedroom across the hall soon enough. She came to the more austere room where her trunk and valise lay.

She closed the door and leaned back against it, trying not to let everything she learned that day cause her to do something rash. As she had told Carter, there was time enough to make plans once Millicent left Forever.

CHAPTER FOUR

The next morning Robert came into the kitchen finding Tess there alone. Sitting, folding his hands in front of him, he began with, "I let it pass yesterday when you said you went out to the Double J in my stead, but we need to come to an agreement about my patients."

"I thought in your advertisement you wanted someone to take some of the burden for caring for patients off your shoulders. Besides, you were hours away and this was an emergency, a cowhand had been gored and was bleeding profusely. It took thirty sutures to close his wounds. I set the leg first as it did not require surgery although the sheriff proved to be a competent assistant. I brought the required anesthetic with me if it turned out to be a compound fracture or there was a need to remove the leg," she explained to her soon-to-be husband.

Robert stood abruptly combing his fingers through his hair saying a little loudly, "That's just what I'm talking about. You are not to perform surgery. You are not to set bones. You are to be my assistant when I need an assistant."

"Let me remind you, Doctor, I performed surgeries alongside my husband in a teaching hospital for a number of years. Then performed them on my own. I became more than proficient and my sutures are well recognized as being some of the best in the states. I do not doubt my ability to handle the patient at the Double

J. If I had doubts, I would have sent for you immediately but then you wouldn't have been able to wait for Miss Phillips to pack and come with you." Tess finished a little spitefully reminding Robert he had been far from worrying about whether a patient needed him.

"I understand that time was of the essence, but in the future, I would appreciate being notified in advance." He combed his hand through his hair again, leaving it standing straight up due to the over use of pomade.

"And I will allow you to handle your patients when you are available to do so." This, if Robert thought about it, wasn't really agreeing to his wishes.

Robert returned a few minutes later and swallowed a little pride when he told her, "Millicent usually likes a cup of tea in bed each morning."

"Well, so do I but I come down here and make it myself. If you wish to wait on your guest, I'm not about to stop you." With that, she picked up her cup of tea and went to take inventory of the medical cabinet to see what she might need to restock.

The midday meal, which Tess usually missed due to seeing patients when she lived in Chicago, was somber. It was the first time downstairs for the lovely Millicent, - and she was lovely. She wore another designer creation with full bustle and yards of extra material pulled up on each side of the waist to cascade down the back and end in intricate flounces around the bottom hem. Her hair was up in curls with a matching ribbon wound through them and pearl-tipped pins holding everything in place.

To say Tess felt rumpled and dowdy was less than accurate. Next to Millicent, Tess felt old, rumpled, and dowdy.

Millicent put on her coat and hat after the meal, saying she must find something decent to read. She would be so long on the stage before she reached a train station to take her the rest of the way to St. Louis and evidently civilization. Robert, of course, offered to escort her since she wasn't familiar with the town, all three blocks of it.

Tess cleared the table. They had eaten in the dining room again so Millicent's dress would have enough room at the table thought Tess uncharitably. Would it kill the woman to help or even say thank you for the meal? Her next thought was, when did I get to be such a harpy? Am I jealous of a woman whom is more attractive than me? Robert is my fiancé after all is said and done. Millicent will leave and Robert and I will marry and I will begin my new life.

Tess had just sat down to do a little crocheting to keep her suturing muscles nimble when there was a rap on the door. She opened it to find a middle-aged couple, their faces creased in worry. The man was helping to hold up a boy of about ten years old, the youngster's flushed face telling of fever and pain.

"Bring him right in here and tell me how he's been feeling and behaving," Tess said as she led the way to the examination table.

"He's been sick, real sick," said the worried mother fussing around the boy as he was laid on the examination table.

The father furnished better symptoms. "First, couldn't get him out of the privy then if'n he even drank water it would come back up. Been that way for more'n a day now."

"What's your name son?" Tess asked to check the patient's cognitive abilities.

"Joseph, Ma'am," he answered and winced as she began pressing gently on his abdomen.

"Isn't the doctor here, Ma'am? I'd feel better if'n he took a look at my boy," the father said.

"I am hoping he will be back soon, otherwise I'll send one of you to get him. He just went to buy some books," she said stretching the truth a little.

"I can do that, Ma'am." Slapping his hat back onto his head the father left.

"What do you think is wrong with my boy, Ma'am? He's my oldest and I don't think I can lose another one. His sister died of somethin' last winter, only five she was. I don't want to bury another child. That's why my husband brought us here today. We didn't call the doctor for my daughter, too expensive we thought. Then we lost her. No amount of money is worth losing a child over," she said dabbing at her eyes with the thin cape she wore over her work dress.

"Medical care is free in Forever as long as I'm here. Never hesitate to come to me when you're ill," Tess said standing up, concerned for the diagnosis she came to.

Robert arrived and tossed his hat toward the sofa as he passed. "What do we have here? A boy with a tummy ache, I hear. Eat too many green apples?" he said cheerfully and listened to the boy's heart with a stethoscope just as Tess had but failed to listen to the abdomen.

Robert reached for a narrow brown bottle. "I think he'll be all right with a little time. I'll send you home with some cod oil tonic. The discomfort should pass in a few hours."

"Doctor Waverly, may I consult with you please," Tess said quietly.

"As soon as I send the patient on his way, Mrs. McLeish," he replied as politely.

"No, before then. I would like to consult with you," Tess said more firmly.

With a smile at the still worried couple, Robert capitulated. "Please excuse us. My assistant is new with my system." Taking Tess by the elbow he steered her into another room.

"What is it? You are undermining the confidence these people have in my ability," he whispered fiercely.

"I do not agree with your diagnosis," she hissed, making sure their conversation didn't reach the other room. "I've spent more time with the boy and he is showing all the symptoms of having appendicitis, an inflammation of the bowel."

"Why does everything come down to surgery with a surgeon? Why can't the boy merely have an upset stomach?" hissed Robert in return.

"Because he has a high temperature. Because his body voided everything he ate or drank in the last forty-eight hours. Because he has tenderness to the right quadrant of his abdomen. Because it hurt to lift his right leg but not the left. Because I have seen over fifty cases of inflamed appendix and this one is classic."

Then she paused to see the doubt of his diagnosis cross Robert's face and finished, "Sending him home in a wagon that will bounce him all over the place will probably cause the appendix to rupture. He'll die painfully within a matter of hours." She watched the emotions flash across her fiancé's face again.

"We'll let the parents decide." He turned towards the door to present his case.

After Robert told the parents what he thought the problem was and Tess presented her prognosis, the father said, "I'll just be takin' my boy home then. Thanks, Doctor. What do I owe you?"

Before Robert could give an amount, the mother said forcefully, "We ain't movin' him, Roy. I know when a child has a tummy-ache and this ain't a tummy-ache. I know this is much worse. After we lost Molly, I swore I wasn't going to lose another child. He stays here and he has the surgery." She glared at her husband with determination and the stance of a bull readying for a fight.

First, there seemed to be the will to argue then the man folded. "If you think that's what he needs, then that's what he gets. It's not that I don't love the boy, you know. It's jist I don't want him sick. A boy lives through a little tummy-ache, I don't know about this here 'surgery'."

Tess sent them to the kitchen and told the wife to fix whatever she wanted for herself and her husband. Then she hurried to prepare the child and room for surgery.

"I take it you'll be able to assist me then, Doctor? I'll need someone to administer the anesthetic. I have the wire cage and things you'll need."

"Certainly, Mrs. McLeish. I await your instructions," Robert said graciously. Now that he didn't need to make the decisions, he was amiable to her taking over the lead role.

Tess calmed her patient, explaining why he was going to go to sleep, but when he woke up, he would be in less pain and have a scar he could show off to his friends.

Robert lit more lamps and got the tray ready for Tess's use although she checked it before she made her first incision. They were both wearing clean aprons, caps, and sleeve-covers up to their armpits. All the latest concepts for surgery from the Chicago teaching hospital Tess was associated with.

Once the boy was undressed and lying sedated to the world, Tess wiped the antiseptic over the area she would be cutting into, leaving a brown stain in her wake. Taking the sharp bladed scalpel, she made an incision and clamped open the area to be able to see the discolored, swollen, puss-filled bowel extension causing all the problems. Tess tied it off then gently cut it free. She carefully removed the infected part before it could burst and spread its venom throughout the boy's body.

As she was making her small, renowned sutures, Robert said apologetically, "I was wrong. I would have killed this child. How come you were so sure? I wasn't with my diagnosis, yet I was prepared to argue with you simply to be seen as right."

"One of the things I learned working with my late husband is there are multiple symptoms on every patient. Many times, the first diagnosis you reach isn't necessarily the correct one. Keep all the symptoms in mind and find the problem that would be the culprit for most of them." She added in a lighter vein, "I have also seen appendicitis and the symptoms were all too familiar."

Robert seemed relieved enough to smile. "I'll tell his parents he's going to be fine now. And as soon as he's awake, they can talk with him."

"I'll finish up in here. He'll need to stay with us for a few days until I'm sure he won't be injured getting home." She took out one of the nightshirts from the bottom drawer and slid it over the boy's head to make him more comfortable as he woke from the sedative.

CHAPTER FIVE

It was the town's busiest week for ailments after the news of the surgery spread. Many of the ladies in town, which really were few in numbers, wanted to meet and be treated by the new woman doctor. Most of her patients' concerns were centered on female complaints they were too embarrassed to consult with the young handsome Doctor Waverly about, but easily handled and cured by Tess. No men showed up to check out the new woman doctor so Tess had plenty of time to keep the house clean, cook the meals, and bake bread.

Robert, on the other hand, took advantage of Tess being in the office to drive Millicent into the country to see spring arrive or visit some of the other ranches. He did check on Tess's patient out at the Double J where Mrs. Wilson entertained Millicent with tea, cakes and some mediocre piano playing according to Millicent at dinner that evening.

"That sounds nice. She was trying to amuse you. You must keep in mind, she didn't have much time to prepare," Tess told the unappreciative younger woman.

"I know but there simply isn't anything to do." Millicent complained for the fiftieth time in the last two days. Evidently, the novel experience of having a handsome doctor at your beck and call wasn't enough of an entertainment any longer.

Tess, enjoying the thought of having Robert and the house all to herself, said, "I understand from the sheriff that the stage will be in the day after tomorrow. Sooner than you know it, you'll be back home with all your friends and amusements at your disposal."

A glance that Tess had trouble deciphering passed between Millicent and Robert. Regret? Sorrow? Tess wasn't sure if it was for them or for her. Somehow, she felt she was at the center of it for both of them.

Midmorning, Millicent came downstairs as lovely as always, dressed in yet another couturier dress and hairstyle, long ringlets hanging over one shoulder.

"I wanted to speak with you so I waited until I heard Robert leave for his rounds. I know you don't think I'm a very good person - too selfish, too concerned with my own comfort. Robert tells me so every day. He's so good I want to be a better person for him, so he thinks better of me." She sat next to Tess who was crocheting on the sofa.

"I don't think you are a bad person. Merely very young and the only child of an older couple. Your parents want only the best for you. You're a lovely young woman and will eventually have a home of your own to care for, to give some sort of meaning to your life," Tess said rather diplomatically for her.

"I know I get more than I should from people because I'm pretty. I could always make men do whatever I wanted, but not Robert." Tess couldn't hide her expression of disbelief. Millicent added, "Not really. I mean, he finally told me you were in his house because he asked you here to become his wife. He feels he owes you marriage because you sold everything in Chicago and came all this way to do so. But you are a widow, you have already had one husband. Is it so important that you have another?" Millicent picked up the lace-edged hankie ready in her hand and dabbed pitifully at her eyes glistening with unshed tears.

Uncharitably the thought went through Tess's mind. Of course, crying would make this woman seem as if the stars from the night sky had landed in her eyes and the cherry blossoms had kissed her cheeks and…. Oh hell, why was she even trying to fight for Robert against this woman?

As if reading Tess's mind, the younger woman said, "You know you're not bad looking if you would take a little time to fix yourself up. You could attract another man, I'm sure of it. Robert said mail order brides are still the way to find a suitable woman of childbearing age. I take it you're still able to bear children?" Millicent asked not so discreetly.

"Yes, I've got a couple more good years in me," the twenty-five-year-old Tess answered sarcastically.

"Oh, good, that makes it so much easier. I thought I would pass on some of the beauty tips I think you could use." Millicent sat up straighter as if in preparation for a lecture. "First, that terrible rusty brown dress is a horrible color with your pink skin undertones."

"Yes, but it hides the blood stains from working with those pesky bleeding patients." Tess continued to furiously crochet what had been a baby cap into a loose mess of yarn.

"You needn't get mean. I was merely trying to say you do not have to take the first man who sends you an invitation to meet him. You should wear lighter colors and you would look much younger. And you need to tweeze your brows. They're beginning to look like one long hairy caterpillar across your forehead. And although, at one time, you would have been in the height of fashion, I'm afraid that era is long over. It makes you look cross all the time," the younger woman said peering seriously at Tess's face.

"Anything else I should change?" asked Tess, hiding her hurt feelings and wondering for the life of her why she should feel hurt. Millicent was only telling Tess the truth.

"Well, your hair is baby fine and looks good except you should rinse it with water that has a little salt and quarter cup of white vinegar added. It will change the muddy brown so it has lighter tones," Millicent said, pulling small tufts of hair loose from Tess's bun. "And we should cut just a few tendrils around the temples and perhaps the back of the neck so they can escape that too tight bun. Let them frame your face, soften the edges,"

"I don't know," Tess said doubtfully then looked over at the mirror above the dining room table and noticed what Millicent had done so far looked better. "What else did you have in mind?"

"Come with me, I'll show you. It won't take long, I promise." Millicent jumped up pulling Tess behind her.

After an hour or so, they both returned downstairs. When Tess caught sight of herself in the mirror, she smiled and turned to the side, looking at the profile of her new hairstyle set higher on her head with springy soft curls hanging down in tendrils.

"I have to admit, Millicent, you were right about it all. I look much better in this cream blouse and dark skirt. The pearls tucked into my hair make me feel like a fairy princess," Tess said as she walked toward the mirror still admiring the work they had done. "And my eyes, they look so large and open now. I didn't realize how pretty my eyes are."

"And I still think I should send you some hair pieces to match your hair. I simply couldn't live without mine. As I said, I'll send you some long curls and shorter pieces to place under your bun or on top of it. Either way, it makes your own hair appear so much longer without the trouble of long hair." Millicent patted her top curls with one soft, white hand.

"But you gave me those beautiful dresses and once I've hemmed them, I'll have so many nice dresses to wear no one will notice my hair."

"They look better with a corset and padded bustle or cage. The trains are measured to have the added height on the rump." Millicent fluffed the back of Tess's skirt for effect.

"I never wear a corset. You should see what it does to a woman's organs. Pushes them all out of place and hinders the lungs from taking in oxygen," Tess explained seriously.

"I still recommend a little rouge. Everyone is wearing it these days. And never come downstairs without using a fragrance. The mercantile here actually has a nice line of scents. You should find one you like and remember the name of the soap I told you about. It wouldn't be as harsh on your hair as one containing lye. I know they carry that here, too." Millicent seemed to be checking Tess over like a mother hen.

"Thank you for everything you have tried to do for me, Millicent. I appreciate it even if I never have time to do everything you've told me about." Tess walked into the kitchen to start fixing dinner.

By the time Robert was home, the house smelled of dried-apple pie and steak prepared ala Swiss. The table as usual was set with the best china and Tess was sitting in the parlor with Millicent.

Robert saw Millicent first, or looked for her first and said his hello then turned to Tess to tell her about a couple of his patients when he seemed struck dumb. "I, why I, did you do something with your hair? I mean, something new?"

"Yes, Millicent was kind enough to help me find a new style," Tess admitted not pointing out all her repaired flaws.

"How nice of her. She really has a lot of knowledge about those sorts of things and, of course, about the opera and art museums. She tells me there are parties and dances every night if one wanted to attend them in St. Louis. Dozens of restaurants too, with French chefs." Realizing he must sound like a tour guide, he added, "But it smells wonderful in here, too. You are a very good cook, Tess, I can't fault you that."

"Dinner will be ready in a few minutes. I'll call you as soon as the potatoes are mashed." Tess got up and saw as she passed the mirror, the reflection of Robert's head leaning nearer to Millicent's with whispered words.

The three ate their dinner and Robert asked cordially of his guest, "Everything packed for tomorrow then, Millicent? Excited to see your mother again, I presume."

"Yes, she and I are very close. We love to shop together and she is a great aficionado of the opera and theatre. We attend every weekend evening when they're in season. It will be so much more enjoyable with…ah, with being back home." She ended lamely, appearing distressed as she glanced at Robert.

"Sounds like you and your mother will have a grand time," Robert said as he forked another bite into his mouth.

When Tess finished the dishes and cleaned-up the kitchen, she went into the parlor where Millicent was just saying goodnight to Robert. "I thought I should get an early night since I'm travelling tomorrow. I appreciate all your hospitality Tess. I assure you I hold you in the highest esteem. Your education, abilities, and integrity put me to shame," the younger woman said sincerely before going upstairs.

Tess was surprised and pleased with the farewell. She was also glad Robert heard someone say something positive about her. After all, she couldn't blow her own horn so to speak, but how else was one to make sure the man she was to marry was aware of her finer points?

"I, too, have to add my esteem of you and your abilities. I find that when I sent for you, I wasn't aware of how proficient you were. I heard of your husband and your father before him but you have the talent of both. As Millicent said, you put me to shame," Robert said quietly, looking serious, too serious for an evening chat.

"I had good teachers, perhaps great teachers, but I can teach you the same techniques. We will get better together," Tess said smiling at his earnest face.

"I don't think that is going to happen, Tess," he said sadly. "I find I have fallen in love with Millicent." As Tess's world collapsed, he continued, "I didn't mean to. I didn't want to, but there it is, I have. I plan on leaving on the stage with Millicent to meet her mother and see if there can be some sort of compromise for us, Millicent and me. She has made it abundantly clear she could not abide living in Forever and I'm not sure I can live in a town like St. Louis. But I'm willing to try if it means she and I can be together."

There was silence, both people thinking. Tess couldn't believe how the last few moments changed their lives completely.

"Do you want me to leave then? When you do?" Tess asked calmly knowing she was the interloper.

Robert jumped up saying quickly, "No, oh, no. I thought it would be best if you kept the practice open. I let my patients know you would be here if they needed anything. I'm not sure for how long. I could possibly sell the practice to a young doctor looking for a quiet town to start in." He wrung his hands he was so distraught. "Actually, I haven't thought that far ahead. I didn't know I was going to leave Forever until recently, believe me."

Pacing, he combed his fingers through his hair. "I thought I could say a proper goodbye to Millicent and go on as we had planned, but found I couldn't face not being near her."

He looked at Tess saying, "You must understand? You must have loved your husband so you know how difficult it would be to let Millicent leave without me."

"Yes, I understand how difficult it must be to leave someone you love. I will see you in the morning then. Pack you both a meal for the road. The stagecoach stops on this side of Austin are of rather poor quality. Millicent may not find anything she would eat."

"That is quite descent of you, really it is. You are taking this better than I thought you would after everything we planned," He couldn't meet her gaze, his eyes moving to first one thing then another.

"Don't worry. My husband also taught me to be flexible since practicing medicine isn't a game that follows concise rules. You need to handle the veritable that always occur." Head held high she ascended the stairs like a duchess.

Abe came to collect the large mound of trunks, cases, and satchels waiting on the front porch of the doctor's office. Tess wasn't planning on walking the couple to the station so said her goodbyes and good wishes for their future in the privacy of the parlor. As soon as she heard the stage move out of town, she went to the back porch and sat in the chair there and cried as if her last friend had left her. The sad part was that last friend had been Millicent.

CHAPTER SIX

Tess knew word had travelled after Robert and Millicent left that anyone needing to see a doctor, would have to see the female doctor. Tess continued office hours, which were pretty much anytime someone knocked on her door.

One day a man in a considerable amount of pain from the way he was walking came to the house and asked, "You the lady doctor?"

At Tess's nod, he said, "I was trying to treat this m'self. I mean it's kinda personal and I heard there weren't no man doctor in town, but I can't stand the pain no more."

"Well, why don't you tell me about the pain. When did it start?" she asked trying to appear unconcerned she may be conversing about a venereal disease this poor man picked up at a honky-tonk.

"I'm not sure, cuz I thought I was jist getting a little saddle sore. I'd been out beatin' the bushes for strays. Gotta get the calves in to be branded an such." His gaze never rose above her neck. "So, I could reach far enough to put some liniment on it. Works great for the horses when one comes up lame."

Tess nodded as if she knew the liniment he was talking about and asked, "I take it the liniment didn't work."

"It seemed to at first but then I went to use it again and I dang near climbed a tree with the shock and pain of it. I don't know what to do. I can't ask one of the other fellers to look at my, ah, you know, man parts, but I'm not too comfortable lettin' you get a look at 'em either." He was now bright red and deeply uncomfortable being around her.

"My husband was a doctor and I understand the need for a male to, umm, handle some conditions, but unfortunately he passed a couple of years ago, so now there is only me. I can attest I am capable of helping you with this pain. It isn't something I won't know how to treat, I'm sure," she confided to the still blushing man.

"If'n yor sure, Ma'am. I can't stand the pain no more." Now that she had explained she was a widow he seemed a little more comfortable with her.

"If you could drop your trousers and bend over the table here, I'll not look at anything I don't need to," she assured him as he did as she asked, his neck an even brighter red.

"I see the problem, sir. You have a tick bite that has now become infected. The tick is still under the skin and it is festering around it. The liniment probably killed the tick but it didn't fall off. Instead, it became imbedded. This will hurt a little before it feels better."

"Them damn ticks. Oh, beg your pardon, Ma'am. We run into them all over the place some times of the year. Never had one fester though," the man explained, his color becoming more normal as he accepted her aid.

"All right then, I'm going to use tweezers to remove the body of the tick and some of the infection. Then I have a nice soft pad with a drawing-salve that will help with the rest of the infection and aid the sore to heal. Come back if it gives you any more trouble," she told him, explaining every step she was doing to his body.

When the man was able to cover himself properly, he said, "Well, that hurt like hell, but you were right about it feeling better already. Thank you, Ma'am. What do I owe you?"

"I'm still new at this part. Leave whatever you think is fair. It didn't really take very long although from your end of things it probably seemed like hours." When he looked at her blankly, she asked, "Does a quarter seem fair?"

"I don't see the doctor often but that sounds fine to me. I'da paid five times that to stop the pain." He placed his hat on his head and tipped it before leaving.

The cowhand was followed through the week by other little ailments. Mrs. White, from the boardinghouse, came when a toenail became infected after kicking a bed frame. The grocer's son fell out of a tree and got a large bump on his head but no concussion. Even Abe from the stagecoach office came in with a nasty gash from a nail on one of the crates he handled. He had sat patiently while Tess placed six neat little stitches in his arm.

Tess felt pretty good about her week's work and sat on the back porch, watching the sun go down. Looking over to the sheriff's house, she saw he was striped to the waist, washing his under arms then his torso. She was mesmerized by the long strokes he made over his tan skin, the muscles bunching and stretching as he washed then rinsed each portion of his body.

She realized she was staring when he went to push down his trousers to bare the rest of his body for ablutions. Lowering her gaze, she moved quickly into her darkened kitchen, making her way upstairs feeling the heat of a blush on her face.

She chided herself for her foolishness. She had seen naked men as cadavers, during surgeries and examinations, at much closer quarters. Why should this man be so much more interesting to her? He was attractive and an excellent specimen of manhood, but would that make her heart beat faster merely thinking of him becoming naked in front of her?

Taking off her dress, she decided to make it an early night again. There wasn't much to do once the sun went down. She thought back at her much busier life when she was married - office hours, surgeries and follow-up care, dinners out and giving lectures in the evenings. She was always moving, always in the midst of men who were highly regarded in their fields. She missed that in a way, the sharing of knowledge and being able to discuss things of interest to her with another adult.

In the morning, Tess stripped her bed of the sheets and grabbed her towel, taking them downstairs to be washed. Now that she lived alone again, there wasn't much laundry. She ran into the sheriff in the backyard. Tess felt the blood rush to her face when she thought about the last time, she saw him.

"Doc, I got this nice jackrabbit, but as I've told you I'm not much of a cook. I was hoping you would find it in your heart to fry this up for us for supper if it ain't too much trouble." He held up a large dressed rabbit.

Tess's mind soared at the thought of having someone to dine with but quickly stamped it down. "I'll cook your rabbit for you but you don't need to share it. You can pick it up this evening."

The smile left the sheriff's face. "I was hoping to talk with you a little. Robert and I used to talk every once in a while. He wasn't one for going down to the saloon, either, and there isn't much else to do in the evenings."

"Certainly then, I accept your invitation for me to cook your meal." She smiled to take the sting out of the teasing. "Come over when you're done for the day."

Tess went inside after hanging up the sheets and began the flour mixture for coating the rabbit. She covered the meat in a marinade and would fry it like southern style chicken, later. Finding root vegetables left from the winter, she added those to the menu. She realized she hadn't cooked a real meal for herself since Robert and Millicent left. Simply ate what was available, wallowing in self-pity. It was time to change that, she thought.

Sheriff Carter came over, his hair wet from his dipping it to clean up for supper. He hung his hat on the peg by the kitchen's backdoor. A warm feeling went through Tess when she saw such a masculine thing in her home.

"Is it alright if we eat in the kitchen? I hated to clear out the dining room now that it's back to being used as a waiting room," she explained to the man who was pulling out a chair to sit on it backwards, setting his arms along the back and watching his hostess.

"I like this better. I think. I can watch what you're cooking and we can talk while you finish up. Unless there's something you want me to help with?"

"No, I've got it all under control. I learned to do it alone when Robert and Millicent were here."

"I'm glad you brought that up. Want to tell me what happened? I expected wedding bells. Then the next thing Abe tells me is Robert's left town with Major Phillip's daughter. It didn't make sense to me. You were so perfect for him. Didn't you think you'd suit?" he asked, seemingly interested in her answer to his question.

"The question never came up, I'm afraid. I was replaced before I even arrived. Robert is a good man but he fell in love with Millicent. He couldn't see himself living here with me when his heart was elsewhere. I don't blame him, I suppose, but it leaves me with a problem."

"How so?" he asked turning the chair around to face the table as she brought the food over and sat down.

"Let's enjoy supper, please. I don't want to re-hash old news." She took a piece of the golden fried rabbit as he did the same.

Carter stood up and carried the plates and flatware to the sink, turning to get the hot water off the stove. Tess put away the extra food, placing it in a pan for Carter to take home. After the kitchen was back in order, the two went onto the back porch. Carter waved her into the rocking chair while he leaned against the railing, bracing his long legs out in front of him.

Tired of watching Tess beat herself up over this, he blurted out, "It wasn't your fault, you know, Tess. Robert had already made up his mind when he brought Millicent home with him. Before he even knew you were here."

"I should have realized from his letters. There must have been something there, some warning that Robert wasn't ready to marry a woman he never met."

"I think Robert was ready to make a commitment when he was writing you, but that all changed when he met Millicent. Someone he never would have met here in Forever under normal conditions. Fate, I guess, if they really are a love match. But you understand that, I'm sure," Carter said, wishing he had a cigarette.

"My husband and I were not a love match although he was a very kind and caring man. He was a contemporary of my father, another doctor." She smiled at how that must sound. "My father died right before my last year in medical school. I had to quit because my father had been my only source of income. Doctor McLeish was one of my professors and offered me marriage as a balm toward what he felt he owed my father." She became quiet as she must be remembering that time. "Then he moved us to Chicago from the University of Michigan's medical school. He was certain we would find a cure for tuberculosis. Doctor McLeish thought he could cut out the tuberculosis, cut away some of the lung and possibly even transplant lungs from cadavers into living people, giving patients lungs they needed to continue to breath. I was his assistant."

"Sounds like a big job for a little woman."

She scoffed but smiled. "We worked with a lot of illnesses. Tuberculosis was only one small part of it. My husband pioneered a new surgery for breast cancer and I worked on the anesthesia to make it more painless. Up to a few years ago, surgeons would remove a woman's breast without any pain relief at all.

It was pure butchery. Now we can save a woman's life and not bring her more agony than the cancer would have."

"That seems a noble venture. Why aren't you satisfied with that accomplishment alone?" The more he heard about this woman the more he grew in awe of her.

"There is so much suffering and death, both of which I feel a need to lessen. I learned a great deal from my father and then my husband. I want to keep learning and growing as a medical expert." He knew, right then, he would support her in any way he could here in town.

He watched the passion for her work pass across her face and asked, "So what's the problem?"

"I never graduated. I never received my degree. It didn't matter as long as I was working beside my husband or here as I worked alongside, Robert. Without a doctor to work with, I shouldn't do surgeries. I don't know what I will do if I get another case like the Johnson boy. I won't let him die. I know that much."

"Sounds like there could be a big problem, Doc."

"Don't call me that. I just told you I don't have a degree," she said crossly.

"You are a doctor. I don't need to see a degree to know that. I saw you work out at the Double J and that work was from a full fledge doctor."

"But if I perform surgery, basically I'd be breaking the law. I'll need to return to university to get my degree. I've decided to write the dean of the medical school I attended and ask if I would be allowed to return. If I can, I need to know what classes would be required to finish my degree. It might take as long as two years if I must re-take any of the other classes. But then that leaves this town without any medical care, not even a midwife."

He could tell she had been worrying over this since Robert left and it was eating her up. "When would you be leaving?" he asked quietly.

"In the fall when the next sessions begin again. I have the funds and I know I can do the work, but I'm a widow and there was a taboo of having married female students before. They may not accept me because of that fact alone."

Now the real problem that she faced was finally in the open, the real fear she kept hidden from him, from everyone. There had been no one to discuss this with before.

"Two years. Seems like a long time but in the big picture it's like a blink of an eye. You'll be back with us in no time. I take it you do plan on returning to Forever?"

He found himself holding his breath as if the answer meant a great deal more than it should for a man whose aspiration was to be the sheriff of a sleepy little town.

"Yes, I do unless Robert finds a doctor to buy his practice. If that happens, I might not need to go back for my degree if the doctor would be willing to have me work with him, but there aren't many patients for two fulltime doctors. I don't know why Robert thought he needed an assistant." Smiling up at Carter, she said, "Perhaps I should knock on wood. I don't want to bring on a landslide of accidents or anything."

He straightened quickly. "I thank you for the fine dinner, Doc, but I know I have an early morning. You can never be sure of yours. I'll take myself home now."

Carter sauntered across the space between the two houses and reached for the tobacco pouch on his back porch for that much-needed smoke. Lighting the hand-rolled cigarette, he inhaled like a man taking a deep breath after being submerged under water. It took a minute but the tobacco did its job and he was less restless and fidgety, able to stay in his own skin.

All those sensations assailing him as he talked in the dark with his attractive neighbor now settling to something he could control. As long as he had thought of her as Robert's intended, he didn't have a problem with her living next-door. Of her sitting on the back porch watching him bathe or standing in her kitchen window doing dishes. Now all that had changed and she was an attractive, unattached woman, experienced with the needs of a married woman and possibly missing that physical closeness with a man.

Closeness he was having a difficult time not imagining between the two of them. He could tell she never wore a corset, the slight jiggle when she dusted the pieces of rabbit with flour fixing dinner and the tightening of her nipple when she plunged her hands into the dishwater. His mouth went dry thinking of how close he had been to brushing against the side of a breast as he helped dry the dishes this evening.

Hell, he'd have to smoke another cigarette if his thoughts kept straying to those sorts of memories. But he had plenty of tobacco and he had too damn much time to think. Looking over to the house, he could see the lights extinguished as she made her way to the entry then the slight glow through the windows of Robert's room as she reached the top of the stairs. Then darkness. She must have entered her own room and closed the door. She wouldn't have turned out the lamp this soon. That would mean she undressed in the dark and he didn't think she was a woman who was ashamed of her body.

He rolled and lit the second cigarette as he thought about her body, full breasted and narrow waist, made for loving with the cradle of her hips just wide enough for a man to nestle into. He felt the erection he'd been trying to deny find more space to expand and inch its way to full-blown desire.

Hell, the state of Kentucky wouldn't have enough tobacco to ease his need tonight. Why did he let this one little woman throw his self-control so out of balance? He didn't understand his body lately. There were just as pretty of women in Jefferson to take a man's mind off work and they were women who knew how to please a man, make sure he got his money's worth.

Tess, for all her being a widow, didn't show any signs of flirting. Or stroking a man's ego or flipping her skirts in his direction although he tried giving her ample opportunity. She treated him as a friend, not a bad start over all, he thought. It could be worse and besides he didn't really want to start something with the woman.

After all, what happens when the need wears off. How would he continue to live right next door when she moved on? Or she could get too clingy. Jealous if he came back home late at night. Make a scene at the city council meeting if he lost interest.

Carter stood and tossed the half-smoked cigarette into a tin can on the porch there for that purpose. No, the right thing was to come home and not instigate anything with the neighbor. Less complications, less chance of hurt feelings and resentment when it was over, less danger. Taking one more long-look at the now dark house next door, he scuffed his boots on the back mat before entering his home.

CHAPTER SEVEN

Tess sent the very important letter off to the dean. Now she felt on pins and needles waiting to hear back, whether she would up-root her life and return to that of a student. She knew academia moved slowly and told herself not to plan on seeing an answer sooner than midsummer when all new students would be notified of their acceptance or denials.

Instead, Tess tried to bury herself in her work. One afternoon a very worried woman brought in her husband. Both were older and the woman was leading her husband as if he had difficulty negotiating the doorways. As the man was finally sitting in front of her, Tess realized his face was distorted and his eyelid droopy. He kept putting a handkerchief up to his mouth to catch the drool that continued forming there. Tess smiled and introduced herself to the couple then proceeded to ask a few questions.

"When did this paralysis begin?" she asked as she took his pulse and listened to his heart, checking with the back of her hand for a temperature.

"This morning, Ma'am," he said with a little bit of a lisp from the inability of his lips to meet.

"Have you been ill prior to this?" she continued to ask questions to ascertain his mental facilities and ability to speak.

The wife was holding a hankie up to her mouth and trying to keep the tears at bay but she couldn't prevent herself from asking, "Is it a stroke? Is my husband gonna die from a stroke?"

Tess turned and looked at the frightened woman and assured her, "No, not today, at least, but I have a few more questions." Turning back to her patient she continued, "Any influenza lately? Ear aches or pain down the side of your neck?"

The man looked surprised and answered, "Yes, as a matter of fact it was hurting me enough, I couldn't sleep the past night or two. How did you know?"

"Well, the good news is this isn't a stroke although I can see why you would think that since it mimics some of the physical aspects. I believe you have a case of Bells Palsy, which should subside within a couple of weeks." Tess included the wife in her conversation. "It is a scary ordeal to go through."

"So, it isn't something he'll die from? He can come home with me?" the wife asked relieved as Tess nodded. "Oh, Calvin, I'm so glad. I was so worried you were going to leave me."

Tess continued, "I'll give you some eye-drops to keep your eye from getting dried out. Everything should be back to normal in about two to three weeks. The paralysis may be with you for as long as six-months although I don't think yours will be. It will be a little annoying but totally non-life threatening."

The wife was letting tears of happiness escape as she helped her husband up and walk toward the front door saying, "How can we thank you, my dear. This has taken a weight of worry off my shoulders."

"There will be no charge for the visit. I will be here if you need me for anything else or if these symptoms change or become worrisome," Tess told them as they left.

Tess was beginning to meet all the town's citizens by their office visits or at Sunday services. The minister, the Reverend Miller, and his unmarried sister, Meredith, were welcoming and had invited Tess into their home for Bible study on Wednesday evenings as well to a few Sunday suppers.

Tess laughed with Meredith, the spinster sister who wasn't much older than Tess, about how the tables should be turned. That Tess should be cooking supper for Meredith and her brother.

"I don't know why it is, but we rarely get invited out. I keep telling the Reverend," Meredith never referred to her brother by his given name, "that he would probably be a married man by now if I weren't here. All the single women would take pity on him and invite him home to supper more often."

"I don't understand the reasoning they are using. Your brother is very attractive and kind and would be a good husband. Just because you're in his home shouldn't affect their feelings." Tess spoke her mind as the two walked from the rectory.

"So, it wouldn't stop you from marrying the Reverend?" Meredith asked looking for any reaction from Tess.

Tess stopped and said quickly, "I wouldn't make a very good minister's wife. I have my own practice, my own career and a minister needs a helpmate, someone who can dedicate her life to his life's work. I'm not looking to remarry although I think any other woman would be a fool to pass him by."

Meredith appeared disappointed with Tess's answer. "I was merely hoping. I mean I know the Reverend holds you in the highest regards and I feel like you are almost a sister already. I could live separately, I guess. Possibly return living with my Aunt Mary in Austin. That might allow the women here to look at my brother in a different light."

"I don't think that would make a difference in a woman's feelings. The rectory is large and there should be room for all of you. What I would like to see is for you to put yourself first and not worry about your brother so much. Have you ever invited a single man who interested you to Sunday supper?"

"Oh, Tess, I couldn't do that. What would he think?" Meredith placed both gloved hands to her blushing cheeks.

"He would think you were interested in him if he wasn't a total block-head. And it would show the women in town that your brother may be needing a helpmate and wife."

Then realizing her friend was mortified at the thought of having a beau, continued a quiet walk to the mercantile where they were going to pick out yarn to make mittens to pass out to the town's children next Christmas.

"Do you think a man would agree to attend a Sunday supper?" Meredith asked just before they entered the store.

"You are a lovely, wonderful woman, who by the way, cooks very well. Of course, there are men willing to come to supper, even with your brother playing gooseberry."

Meredith took the comment seriously. "Oh, I couldn't entertain a man without a chaperone."

"I agree, so it would not be a surprise to your guest that your brother would be there, too."

When Tess arrived home, she went directly to her sewing bag to work on her knitting once again but thought things were out of place. She always arranged her needlework a certain way to prevent the threads from becoming tangled. This time things looked different so she did a more thorough search and found her sewing thimble missing. Tess always put it in the same place, but now it was nowhere in the bag. She emptied the basket completely, even shaking it upside down. Her pack of needles was no longer in the side pocket and the tool used to remove a hem fell out. It was always kept in a leather case. That was strange. And although Tess hadn't been in the bag for a couple of days, she was sure she had not left it in that condition.

Upstairs, Tess noticed her bed was messed, but as she got closer, she realized what she first thought were random wrinkles was actually a print of buttocks on her coverlet. She automatically smoothed it out then questioned how it got there. Tess always sat in the chair in the corner to put on her shoes so why was the bed's cover messed?

While on the back porch, Tess called over to Carter as he walked from his house towards the street using the wide path between their two homes. "Did you notice anyone over here this afternoon, Sheriff?"

"No, so you think you missed a patient?" He stopped moving in the direction of the jail and walked towards her.

"I am not sure but someone was in my bedroom. Someone sat on my bed."

Concern filled his face. "Can I see your room? Maybe it will make more sense to me then."

Tess didn't hesitate, completely at ease with the sheriff now after all their time spent together. "I sleep in one of the rooms on the opposite side as this. I still leave Robert's open in case he returns."

Carter's mouth turned down at that information but didn't say anything, simply continued into the house, leading the way upstairs. "You still leave the door unlocked during the day like Robert did?" At her concurrence, he finished saying, "Maybe it's time not to be so accommodating. I mean you're an attractive woman and if people, well men, knew you weren't behind locked doors it might give them some ideas. Let's be on the side of caution here and lock the front door even in the daytime."

Tess seemed to be trying to find rational explanations, probably not wanting to live under a police state behind locked doors. "I may be completely wrong. I may have sat on the bed myself and just forgotten. I suppose the sewing bag could have got knocked over then set up again without me realizing things had been disturbed."

Carter stopped, gazed into her eyes, and asked, "Do you think that's what happened? That you forgot about sitting on the bed or, what did you say, messed-up your own sewing bag?"

Tess gazed at the now neat bed, "No, I am very precise about how I leave things. Doctors have to be because in an emergency I need to know where all my instruments are, even in the dark."

"That's what I thought. So, you say the imprint was where, on this side of the bed?" As she nodded, Carter sat down where the imprint had been. He looked around trying to see what someone sitting there would see. "I can reach this drawer. What's in it?"

Tess felt her face redden a little as she explained, "Just my stockings and, umm, under things."

"Open it but don't touch anything until I ask you to."

Once the drawer was opened, he asked her, "Is there anything missing or out of place?"

"I am not sure, but it looks like someone squeezed everything together, like they were going to take it all out at once." Her brows drew down in consternation.

"But nothing's gone, missing?" he asked again. "Go ahead and go through the items."

When Tess did what he asked, she said, "No, everything's here. I don't bother having a lot of things at one time. When I need more, I'll get more. I have three sets of winter stockings and three sets of summer stockings and three camisoles. My underskirts and dresses are hanging up along the wall and they all seem to be there." As she looked around the room at the washstand and her brush and soap dish, she didn't see anything missing.

Carter stood and asked, "All these rooms used up here? I mean they have furniture and stuff in them?"

"Yes, even the box room at the end of the hall has my luggage in there now, but was filled before Robert left and took his trunk and cases." They descended to the foyer.

"Where's this sewing bag?"

Tess pointed to the large quilted bag on the floor leaning against the end of the sofa. Carter didn't take long to look it over and its position. "Do you have anything like laudanum or opium here?"

Tess raised her hand to her mouth. "I didn't even think to check them. Some people are very addicted. I should have thought about theft when I first thought an intruder was here." She hurried into the examination room to exhale the breath she was holding. "Nothing's been touched in here. I would swear to it." She smiled in relief.

"That's a shame. I'd feel a whole lot better if the fellow got what he wanted and left. Now I feel you're the target and I don't like the thought of some man watching you, waiting for you to leave so he can go through your personal things." His mouth formed a firm line and his gaze hardened.

"Why would anyone do that? Why think a man would be interested in me at all? I'm a dowdy, homely widow. How desperate would a man have to be to be interested in me?" Tess questioned honestly.

Carter looked at Tess and became angry with her complete disbelief that a man, that anyone, would find her attractive. He laid the blame for that at Robert's feet. The doctor had undermined whatever confidence this woman had and that infuriated Carter.

"You're a warm beautiful woman. How any man could take you for granted is beyond me. I get hard for you every time I'm closer than ten feet, every time I look over here and find you sitting on the porch in your nightclothes." Carter admitted to a rather shocked Tess.

"It doesn't matter really. It happens every time I think of you which is becoming more and more often lately."

Tess stared at the floor not knowing how to answer.

Sorry for blurting out his feelings now, when Tess was worried about intruders, Carter said roughly, "Lock the door as soon as I leave. Be wary if things look out of place again and don't hesitate to call for me if you feel the least bit threatened." His boots made loud thumps as he left through the rear door.

CHAPTER EIGHT

Tess spent more time at home, not that there were more patients but because she felt like she was being watched whenever she walked in town, even on Sunday when she went to church. She would search the house upon arrival home thoroughly for any sign someone had been in the rooms when she was away.

Called out to one of the ranches, she rented a buggy and drove herself to the Rocking R where one of the farriers had gotten kicked by a horse. It missed his head but tore a large gash in his chest and shoulder, just missing the tendons.

"A little higher and I'm afraid you would have lost the use of this arm, Jason. I've done some reconstruction of the chest area, but there will be a good-sized scar. If you follow through with the exercises, I'm leave with you, in a few months you'll be back to having full use of it." Tess packed-up her bag and stood over her patient.

"I can't thank you enough, doctor," the owner of the ranch and father of the injured man said. "I was so frightened when I saw him. I've seen men lose an arm with a lesser injury during the war. What can I do for you? What can I pay you?"

"Well, it cost me a dollar to rent the horse and buggy, that'll make me happy." She wrote out some medical directions for the man to follow prior to his visit to her office in two weeks. "I don't want your muscles to atrophy, get used to being unused for too long. You'll lose strength and the ability to stretch if you baby the arm too much. But, on the other hand, don't do too much or you won't heal and you'll get the same outcome. Stop working the arm when it hurts, do only the number of each movements I wrote out on the sheet. We will increase them as you heal." She stared pointedly into the young man's eyes. "Promise that you are listening to me?"

"I'll make sure he follows your instructions, doctor. He has a habit of thinking he's invincible," his father said and walked out to the buggy with her. "Do you want one of my men to go back with you?"

"No, I know the way now and it won't be dark until after I get home. Now watch him. He'll be woozy for a while with the sedatives, but then he's going to hurt like hell," she told the father honestly. "The laudanum should help, but if alcohol is available its less addictive if he doesn't have a problem with it."

The owner waved her off and Tess turned the buggy neatly driving out of the gate to the main road, being careful to miss the ruts. Part way home she saw a tall horseman riding towards her. The hair on her neck seemed to stand-up and a prickly sensation ran though her body. As the rider got closer, Tess relaxed as she recognized the sheriff's form and face, hidden under his Stetson.

They hadn't spoken since the night she called on him to help with finding the intruder. She found she missed their talks and their shared meals. She wasn't as uncomfortable around him as she would have thought considering he told her he desired her sexually, and often. It made her lower abdomen feel funny. She would need to think about that at another time.

"I came out to escort you back to town but I see I'm a little late. Mind if I tie my horse to the back of the buggy and ride with you?" he asked when they both came to a stop in the middle of the road.

"No, that's fine. I could use a rest. My arms are tired from working with a patient."

"I heard you got called to the Rocking R. No one hurt too bad, was there?" he asked seemingly more to make conversation than nosiness.

"Jason, the owner's son, got kicked by one of the horses he was trying to shod. It nearly tore his arm off at the shoulder. A horse's kick can do as much damage as a cannon shot. They are beautiful animals, but temperamental. I know I never want on the wrong end of one."

"I got kicked hard while in the Calvary. It was a new horse but something told me to move fast and I just got part of what he was passing out. Now, unless I know the horse well, I keep my distance. I respect their rights and needs and give them a wide birth."

"Well, Jason will probably be a little less casual around them, especially the back end of one." She became quiet, enjoying the drive in the country, noting how full the trees were and how some of the flowers were beginning to turn to fruit.

When they arrived in town, Carter dropped Tess off at the doctor's office then took the horses back to the stable. She entered the house and carefully looked for anything out of place.

She had stopped doing that a week earlier. But since she had been gone not only from home, but also from town, she felt she should check things closer. She inspected the examination room when she left her black bag there and all the bottles and jars seemed in the exact same place as usual.

As she went upstairs, she sensed a change. As if someone had been there and not long ago. As if she could feel his shadow as he snuck in and back out, leaving something of himself, some scent of desperation. She went through the empty rooms but found nothing out of place before entering her own where she began to relax.

The bed was smooth and creaseless, the drawers un-opened. Taking off her hat, she placed it next to her hairbrush when that item caught her eye. She picked it up and looked closely. There wasn't a strand of hair in it - and there should have been. She peered around for any other sign someone had been there but the clean brush was the only evidence.

Tess went out to the back porch, unsure whether to tell Carter what she suspected when he came down the path towards his house. "Everything all right?" he asked and veered towards her when he didn't get a quick reply.

"I think, no, I know someone was in my house. Someone took hair out of my brush." At his confused expression, she explained, "I didn't have time to clean the hair out of my brush this morning because I was called out to the ranch. Millicent said I should do so and make a little bundle to use as a hairpiece to give my hair more height. The bundle is in my hair now but the brush is completely empty. It is never empty. I shed like a Shetland pony in spring."

"So, someone came in again while you were gone." He was thinking out loud. "But I suppose any number of people knew you left town from the hostler at the livery, anyone who heard or saw you leave, anyone the cowhand who came and got you might have told. Anyone who came and found your office closed and anyone they might have told. Pretty much covers the whole town," he said sounding frustrated.

"I'm sorry. It's not really important. Perhaps it was a mouse wanting a nice soft nest for its babies. I've heard of that before. I mean mice stealing hair for nests."

"Are there any droppings? Can't have mice without lots of droppings."

Tess shook her head sadly, "No, no signs of mice."

"Then I'll be looking for a little bigger varmint."

"Sheriff, would you like to come to supper? I can fry some ham slices and make red eyed gravy and biscuits," she offered tentatively with a smile.

"That sounds tasty, Doc. You know I don't cook so my can goods can wait another day." He turned back toward his house where he had been heading when she stopped him.

At supper, the long-legged man sat comfortably at the kitchen table with Tess, eating with the concentration of a man with a lot on his mind.

Tess finally needed to ask, "Is there something bothering you, Sheriff?"

"Sorry, I guess I'm not being much of a guest. I was thinking about the last time, the last supper we ate together. Wondering if you've heard anything back about your schooling and if you're still planning on leaving?" He wiped his mouth and placed the napkin next to his empty plate.

"No, nothing yet. I received a letter from Robert saying he was having no luck selling the practice. I don't see a way to continue on as a doctor except for me to get my degree." She stood and took the plates to the dish tub.

"But you still want to return here to Forever?" he asked as if he was unsure, he wanted to know her answer.

"Oh, yes, I'm making friends and getting to know the area. I like living here, even with the limited entertainments. I don't think I will ever want to live in a city again."

"Not even if there were more opportunities to do surgeries or work with other doctors on cures and new procedures? I find that hard to believe." He watched her closely as if her answers were important to him.

"I had that already and I enjoyed working with my husband, but it was the patients I enjoyed most. Helping them live a better life. I really like working with the expectant mothers. There are two of them here and I'm hoping I will be able to deliver their babies yet this summer." She knew there was excitement in her voice. It always happened when she thought about bringing new life into the world.

"Yeah, you would like that. I can see how you could be happy here now with all the different ways you help. You can really make a difference to the lives here." He finished drying the last pan. "I better be off home now. Lock the door after I leave."

Tess locked the door and went to the parlor, too unnerved yet to go to sleep. Sitting down near the one burning lamp, she picked up her knitting. There were a lot of mittens that needed to be finished even if Christmas was several months away.

She thought how easily she and the sheriff fell back into effortless conversation even if he seemed slightly distracted. Not that he ignored her but he was thinking of other things while they ate. Of course, he was the sheriff and many things fell under his domain she was sure. A spinster neighbor wasn't his only concern even in a town this size.

A creaking in the house caught Tess's attention and she stopped the light clicking of her needles to listen. Perhaps she did have mice. Darn, she thought, I hate those things. They carry disease and leave droppings like dirty snowflakes over everything.

With silence in the house her only reward for staying quiet, Tess began the rhythmic motion again fashioning the mitten into some semblance of a hand. She stopped again, sure there had been a slight sound, out of place from the house's usual creaking and groaning. Deciding it was time to go to bed if she was going to jump at every little noise, Tess put away her knitting.

Lighting a candle in the holder from the oil lamp, she turned down the wick until the lamp went out. Walking up the stairs, she lit the lamp on her bedroom nightstand, checking the shadows for hidden danger. She shook her head at her own fancy. If she continued like this, she wouldn't be able to relax and sleep in her own room.

Undressing and hanging her clothes on the pegs, she placed the rolled stockings and shoes next to the chair. Then she felt a sense of unease that seemed to crawl across her skin. This was going to have to end, even if she proved herself a fool.

After pulling on her nightgown, she opened her covers. She then placed pillows so they appeared as if someone was sleeping in the bed and drew the sheet up over the lumps. Pulling on her wrapper, she blew out the candle before moving silently to the chair. She would stay up all night to prove to herself there was no one in the house except, possibly, a frightened mouse. The bedroom door was left ajar as usual and she sat down to spend a boring night listening to non-existent threats.

Tess was about to climb into the inviting bed when she was suddenly aware of a noise, a real noise, in the hallway. Holding her breath, she thought the door opened wider than she had left it. There wasn't much light in the room, only slight moonlight from the uncovered window. Tess always left it uncovered. That way she knew when to get up as the dawn's light came right in to her bed.

She tried to breath quietly but her heart beats were like thunder in her ears, telling Tess she was under stress. She kept her place, not ready to expose herself to the intruder who she was positive was behind the door, hidden from her view.

Then a man came into the bedroom, hunched-over, heading toward the pillows covered with blankets, something held out in his hand, a weapon, a knife. It was pointed and he was approaching what he thought was Tess in the bed.

Tess was mentally kicking herself for not thinking ahead and bringing a weapon but it was too late now. She could be face to face with this intruder and was hoping being caught unawares would be enough to make the man run.

"Who are you and what do you want?" she yelled as she threw a shoe at him.

The man made a yelp of surprise. Dropping his weapon, he turned and ran pulling the door closed behind him.

Tess yanked the door open and was right behind him, but then self-preservation came into play. She tore down the stairs and through the house out the rear door. As soon as the cooler air hit her face, she began screaming for Carter. Yelling his name repeatedly in fear, she smacked into a bare chest as she entered his back porch.

Carter held both her shoulders looking her over, searching for an injury in the pale light of the moon. He was wearing just his trousers, the buckle undone, and the fall opened. "What's wrong, Tess. Answer me." He shook her. Keeping her from going into shock.

"It's, it's him, I know it now. He was in the house, in my room," she said. Her teeth beginning to chatter with her reaction to the fear.

"Stay here and lock the door. I'm going to find that bastard." He pushed her toward his house's door. That's when Tess realized he held his gun in his hand, too.

Tess huddled in the corner of the leather couch, which she had tripped over when she entered. She knew there were lamps nearby but sitting in the dark made her feel safer, able to hide from her threat. She saw a light begin in the kitchen of her home and travel through the downstairs. It disappeared to reappear for a second in Robert's room on the second floor before finally returning to the parlor and going out. Tess did not move. She would wait until she was sure it was the sheriff.

A rap on his own door and a quietly whispered, "Tess, let me in."

Tess walked on stiff legs to the door and unlocked the bolt, opening the door and asking, already knowing the truth, "Did you find him?"

"No, he was gone by the time I got there. Out the front door which I know was locked when I left. I tried to follow him, at least I went down the main street to see if there was a horse tied up or anyone suspicious around. The saloon is in full swing and I looked in to see if anyone looked like they were winded from running, but no one stood out. I asked Abe at the ticket office if he saw or heard anything, but he's there taking inventory before the stage comes in tomorrow morning. He hadn't seen anything since he's been in the storeroom all evening."

"I'm sorry to be such a nuisance. I don't know why I panicked," she said chastising herself for her fear. She should have grabbed the man - except for his weapon.

"Why did you set up your bed that way? Were you expecting him?" Carter asked. His pants and belt were secured, even if his bare feet still showed.

"Not really, but maybe," she answered, giving the sheriff a mixed message. "I was downstairs and I felt I wasn't alone in the house. But then felt foolish because there wasn't a reason for me to suspect anyone else was there."

"So, it was just a gut feeling that saved your life?" he asked nonchalantly but she thought he wanted to ask more.

"I wouldn't say my life was in danger, but I was scared and reacted. I didn't have a weapon and that was foolish on my part."

"Well, he did. I take it you didn't have a long pair of black handled scissors in your room? I found them on the floor near the bed."

"Oh, that's what he was holding. It sounds like one of the pairs I have in the examination room." She sat silently for a moment taking in the information. "You think he was there to kill me then? I've made someone so mad they want me dead?"

She was unable to fathom what she had done since coming to town to make someone want to kill her, well, not anywhere actually.

She had lost patients in Chicago, patients who no matter how hard she tried, she couldn't save. The families were always grateful for the few extra weeks or months she could give them with their loved ones, no one seemed to want to exact some kind of retribution when their family member died. Moreover, the patients she saved certainly wouldn't have a grudge.

"I don't think it's anyone who's rational." Carter's words interrupted her thoughts. "If someone wanted a person dead, a gun is the fastest method. There are more dangerous items in that examination room of yours than a pair of scissors no matter how long or sharp they'd be."

"That's true. There are knives and saws and scalpels. A pair of scissors was more like he was trying to scare me, not cut me."

When she tried to see Carter's expression, she saw the glitter of his eyes as he watched her. She came to the final acceptance. "We have someone who is deranged then. I'm his target but we may not have a direct link between us, merely something in his own mind."

"It appears that way. I'm sorry but I don't have any idea who in town has these tendencies. We will just hope they don't turn more violent." Walking across the room, he returned with a pillow and blanket from a trunk.

"I take it you don't want to return to the house until we can at least make sure he isn't hiding in there."

"You're right about that. I want to have a lot of light before I head into that house again. Sorry for the inconvenience." She accepted the couch as her bed for the night.

"Not much hospitality, I'm afraid. I'd give you my bed but then the hens in town would really have a time of it. If we play this right, no one will know you spent the night here instead of your own bed. G'night." She heard him go into the next room and push the door shut.

CHAPTER NINE

As the sun was coming up, Tess was woken by a gentle shake to her shoulder. She looked up to see Carter, a soft smile on his lips. "I've checked every room and I'm positive there is no one in the house. Do you want me to go back with you?"

"No, you were right last night. I'll go back alone, either one of us leaving the other's house would be a bit more than most of the town could bear. One at a time may not get noticed. After all, I'm a widow and you are one of the few bachelors in town now. I don't want people to think I corrupted you, too."

Responding to his questioning look, she explained, "It's been said I drove Robert away merely to take over his patients. Why disabuse them when Robert may have to come back and start where he left off?" Tess pushed off the blanket and stood in only her gown and wrapper, her hair messed from all the events of the night.

Arriving home, she felt the same security she normally felt within its walls. Going upstairs, she looked around, finding nothing but her shoe out of place and the blankets still over the pillows as she left them. She washed with the cooled water from the night before and dressed as usual, taking a little more time with her hair since she hadn't put it into the normal braid.

She was downstairs and heating coffee when Carter came over, empty cup held out. He didn't even step up onto the porch but said with a grin and a day's growth of beard, "I see you re-styled your hair. I kinda liked the tussled look of you this morning. As if you spent a night in a man's bed."

"Are you actually flirting with me sheriff? I saw what I looked like this morning and tussled wasn't exactly the word I'd have used to describe the rats nest sitting on my head," She liked this teasing flirting man.

"To each his own. Got another cup for me before I go?" He held up the newly emptied cup. Tess refilled it and Carter turned towards his office to begin his day.

That afternoon, Carter showed up at the front door with a wiggling, panting fur ball in need of shearing at his feet. "I thought Buddy here might make you a little more comfortable in the house. He's friendly and house broken and well-behaved - for the most part anyways."

"What's for the most part?" she asked skeptically.

"He barks at strangers like a crazy mutt. Send him to the kitchen or backyard when you have a patient, but he'll let you know if someone is hiding in the house," Carter explained as Tess knelt down and fondled the little dog that rolled onto his back to have his belly scratched, too. "Oh, he's a great mouser. Faster than a cat and will take on a rat or two if you have any of those around the house."

"How could I turn him down? He seems so sweet," she said continuing to pleasure the dog by scratching his ears.

"If he starts to bark at someone you know as a friend, simply tell him 'friend' and he'll welcome them into your home, too." Chuckling, Carter told her, "I'm a little envious of the attention you're giving the dog. After all, I like my belly scratched, too."

Her brows rose as he backed away laughing. "Sorry, I couldn't resist. But Buddy had such a look of ecstasy I had to say something."

Tess looked at the little dog and smiled while visions of chewed rugs and pillows danced though her mind. She took the little dog to the kitchen and found a nice sized bowl for water that she filled and set on the floor by the rear door. Buddy lapped a couple of times then began his patrol of the premises, checking the smells from behind every cupboard and under every door. Tess thought, perhaps I do have mice. He seemed interested in something around there.

The rest of the day was spent with Buddy getting familiar with every room although Tess shooed him out of the examination room as soon as he put a paw into it. Then it was on to the upstairs with again sniffing under furniture and whining until she opened the box room.

That's when she realized the room had been rearranged to accommodate a sitting place for someone. This is where the man waited and hid while she and Carter ate dinner, waited here making plans while she knitted in the parlor, waited until he thought she was asleep and vulnerable.

The antics of the little dog soon took her mind off the intruder. Carter said the pup was noisy when a stranger came too close so Tess would have a warning the next time someone was in the house. She took the dog into the backyard and threw a stick that Buddy returned to her. When he tired of the game, he laid down with his belly flat to the ground and his hind legs splayed as he chewed on the stick, his little tongue licking the pieces of wood dust.

"Oh, no you don't. I can't see that wood splinters would be good for your tummy either. Let's see what else we have for you to teethe on. I may have a joint that should be good," she said and went into the house for the treat.

The next day there was a rap on the front door and just as Carter indicated, the little dog ran to the door in a blur, barking furiously, threatening with everything he had until Tess looked out the sidelight and saw Mrs. White again.

"Friend," Tess told the little dog as she opened the door. The little dog gave a sniff at the visitor then laid down on the bed in the kitchen that Tess had made up for him.

"I wanted to let you know my toe is so much better. I don't think we'll have to take the nail, but you need to look at it for yourself, Dearie," Mrs. White hustled into the examination room and pushed off her slipper.

After examining the once infected toenail, Tess agreed. "I think the acid I used to take down the swollen area has done a better job than I predicted. I think your toe will heal on its own and we won't need to take the nail. Another couple of days and you'll be wearing your shoes again. In time to go to church."

"Well, I'm very happy this is over so soon and without much pain once I visited you. Thank you, doctor." Mrs. White bustled to the front door while Buddy watched quietly from the kitchen doorway.

Tess spent the rest of the morning and early afternoon taking care of the garden she had planted, mostly herbs that were used in home-remedy cures. Tess was well-trained and knowledgeable of the plants used to medicate patients. She would harvest the seeds and dry the plants in the fall for use the rest of the year or until she could have another garden.

If she received the needed college entrance invitation she wouldn't be here. Perhaps she could have a window box wherever she called home for the next couple of years while she finished getting her degree.

She stared at the sheriff's house and a tinge of pain-like ache went through her chest. She was there to marry one man. If Robert came back to Forever, she would honor their agreement. Tess was sure of that.

Then her gaze traveled over to the porch. Memories of sitting in the dark watching Carter strip down and wash after a day's work had other parts of her anatomy becoming active. Not an ache but a yearning, a seeking she had no name for.

The dog's movement drew her attention. Buddy spent his time with his nose to the ground, following long dead trails that hadn't been used by the animal in question for weeks. He found a grasshopper and kept his nose just behind it, making the insect jump and land, jump and land. The dog right on its tail, so to speak.

Wiping her hands together to leave as much of the soil there as possible, she got up, taking the rug she was kneeling on with her. Carter came down the path and Buddy ran to him, jumping up, begging to be petted. Carter squatted and laughed, roughing up the dog's ears with his large hands.

"I have a pot roast on the stove for tonight if you would like to join me," Tess said coming up to the man who seemed to always make her feel better simply being around him.

"That would be much appreciated, Doc. You know I never turn down a meal. Maybe I should drop off a rabbit or ham or something in reciprocation." He was still smiling although Buddy has lost interest in them both.

"I am trying to thank you for helping me with my intruder or whatever. Having Buddy is a great relief and I would never have thought of getting a dog. I was away from home for so many hours of the day when I lived in Chicago, I didn't have a pet. Now I rather like having something to talk to throughout the day."

"Me, too, but I never know when I might get called out for days at a time chasing after rustlers or robbers," he told her finally standing up, making a shade for her there in the pathway.

"Dinner can be ready anytime you are."

"Let me get cleaned up and I'll be right over." She watched as he continued to his house to use the washstand on the porch.

CHAPTER TEN

"Meredith, how nice to see you." Tess welcomed her friend at the door. "Let me clean-up the examination room from my last patient. Then I can stop and have tea with you," Tess said as the little dog barked menacingly from behind Tess.

"Friend, Buddy." The dog immediately calmed and sniffed around the hem of Meredith's skirt then onto the front porch. "Come in, I sometimes forget he's here as a guard dog."

"What do you need a guard dog for?" Meredith asked. "He certainly doesn't look very ferocious now." They both looked over at the fluff of fur playing with a leaf on an overhanging bush.

"Well, he isn't that kind of a guard dog - merely noisy. Sheriff Carter gave him to me to let me know if any strangers were around, you know, possibly attracted by the drugs I have in the house," Tess fabricated. Unable to tell her new friend she had an enemy, but didn't know who it is. "It's because I'm a woman, I'm sure."

"Sheriff Carter scares me, so perhaps it's just as well you have a guard dog." Meredith followed Tess into the waiting room and stopped. "I've come as a patient, well, not me exactly but for the Reverend."

"He isn't feeling well? What seems to be the symptoms?" Tess asked becoming the professional she was.

"He says it's nothing, but he's had this cough for weeks now. We thought it would go away, with the warmer weather but it hasn't." Meredith told her worriedly, "If anything, it seems to have gotten worse."

"Is it at a specific time of day? You know, first thing in the morning or late at night? While lying in bed?" Tess continued asking questions that might help her diagnose the problem without the patient's presence.

"I hear it mostly in the middle of the day and I know drinking a warm drink doesn't do anything for it nor does gargling salt water."

Tess could see how really distressed Meredith was about her brother's condition. "I suppose he doesn't want to come in for an examination? Because I'm a woman and he's who he is?" she asked unnecessarily.

"I'm sorry, Tess. I think it's because he knows you in a personal way, too." Meredith offered, to soften the rejection.

"Tell him I won't need to have him undress. He can remain completely reverend-like while I check his lungs and breathing. You can be with us the whole time." She hesitated then needed to let her friends know how dangerous this could be, so added, "I have seen too many people die of tuberculosis not to feel the need to urge you to bring your brother to me."

Meredith's eyes widened then nodded decisively, "He'll be here if I have to drag him."

"Let's hope it doesn't come to that. Meanwhile, I'm going to give you a cough syrup and if this doesn't help, then I need him in here." Tess went to the cupboard in the examination room and took down one of several clear glass bottles, ones with their corks still sealed with wax.

"Follow the instructions on the back. I'm sorry to have frightened you, but some time it's the simple things that have us catch the more difficult things early."

"I'm due back so I'll have to take a rain-check on the tea. Thank you for understanding, Tess. It's not because he doesn't trust you as a doctor or anything," Meredith babbled as she was leaving.

Tess smiled as she leaned against the door. She never thought about that aspect before. It has been years since anyone of consequence questioned her ability, not since she was first introduced by Doctor McLeish in Chicago. Perhaps she does need to re-establish herself, but she will need that pretty, embossed degree first.

The scratching on the door reminded Tess her furry warrior was on the porch, now locked out of all the fun stuff on the inside. "Come on in and chase the dust motes. I've still got the room to clean-up."

The next day Meredith and Reverend Jenkins, red faced and perspiring, stood in front of Tess as she opened the door.

"Friend, Buddy," Tess quieted the dog, which made things easier all the way around. "Come in, both of you. I'm glad you've decided to seek medical advice, Reverend. A cough can signify many other ailments."

"So, you informed my sister, Mrs. McLeish. The point you made about tuberculosis sat heavily on my mind since I deal with so many of the elderly and ill. I was afraid I would infect them in their weakened conditions. I do hope that is not the case with me or I shall have to give up ministering to my flock."

"Let us hope that is not the case then although in a young healthy person such as yourself, it is controllable and even curable." Tess knew the fear was reasonable. "But it would be months before you would be unable to pass it on to others, especially ones in weakened conditions."

Tess listened to the reverend's chest then thumped him on the back and re-listened. She examined his eyes and asked to put the stethoscope to his neck and ankles then sat on the stool beside the examination table and spoke to them both.

"I don't find any other symptoms of tuberculosis, Reverend. You are very healthy. My concern is that I hear a heart murmur, sometimes a beat so light I almost missed hearing it. I think somewhere in the past you were ill and the heart, which is a muscle, was damaged. Not enough for you to notice, but it was attacked, fought off that attack but became wounded in the fight. That is the best way I can describe it."

Meredith looked at her brother then asked, "Could a severe case of influenza have done this? Last year almost the entire town came down with it and the Reverend tended to the ill whenever he could until he became too sick himself."

"If the cough is new then yes, the influenza could have been the start of the damage. The good news is it shouldn't get worse or cause problems with your continuing to minister to your congregation. I can give you an elixir to ease the cough, but it is something you will always need to contend with. Unfortunately, we've no cure for the heart once it's been damaged." Tess was sorry to pass on this sad truth.

"That I haven't been spreading tuberculosis around my parish is good news to me. The other, I'll pray on and find solace and guidance from above," he said happily. Tess knew he meant every word.

"I am glad you found the time in your busy schedule to come in to see me. It's always a pleasure to talk with you, Reverend. Meredith." Keeping the meeting professional, Tess escorted the couple out to the porch, the little dog following behind them all.

That evening Carter came down the path and held up a paper wrapped package in his hand. "I've got some steaks and I'll share if you'll cook," he tempted teasingly.

"And you'll eat if I cook if I remember the rest of the message," Tess teased back. "Leave them with me and I'll fry them up when you get done for the day. See you later tonight then?"

"Just need to clean up." He cheerfully left the package with Tess and went to his back porch. She fought the urge to watch him out her kitchen window knowing he would be half-naked within her view. Tess forced herself to concentrate on dinner and not on her neighbor.

CHAPTER ELEVEN

The night was more than warm, it was downright hot. The humidity made Tess want to take her clothes off and sleep naked. A dangerous thought combined with the thoughts plaguing her ever since her good-looking neighbor left for home after dinner.

Sitting there at the kitchen table, she watched as his forearms bunched and relaxed with each forkful of food as he lifted it to his mouth. Those firm lips closing over the tines and the fork sliding easily out from between them. The motion of his Adams apple as he swallowed, going down to beneath the collar of his shirt then back into position, where Tess could have reached it to place a soft kiss.

Tess was so mesmerized she missed his asking for the salt for his tomato slices. It took his asking twice before she snapped back to reality and handed it to him. He mistakenly took her lapse as her being tired. He left earlier than usual which was always plenty early anyway. This time he left without their usual talk on the back porch. Not that it was ever that exciting but it was time they spent, just her and him.

Standing by the open window there was nothing moving. The night air was the same temperature as the room - no breeze, no relief. She wiped a cool, wet cloth over her neck and down her breasts, hoping it would lessen her heat, her need. She knew it wasn't only the hot Texas night that kept her awake.

She knew she was in trouble the minute Carter came into the kitchen that evening, his sleeves rolled up to the elbow, one side of his shirt unbuttoned and laying open at the neck. His hair was wet from the dunking he gave it then combed back with his fingers.

His face was freshly washed but there was stubble given that it had been early morning since he had shaved. She had watched him shave from the back porch as she drank her morning coffee, before he brought his empty cup over for her to fill.

He made no apologies for his appearance as he sat down on her kitchen chair before supper and talked about his day, watching her fry the last of the potatoes and turn the steaks. She spent the time devouring him with her eyes and enjoying every morsel. She hoped it didn't show - her avarice, that is. She wanted him to feel comfortable enough to come over for dinner, for talks, for anything.

Hmmm, she had it bad, whatever it was. She had heard and read about it, of course. Never thought she would acquire the same desperate need that controlled other people's lives. Now she could understand why some people were driven to do things they would never contemplate when they were rational. This want, this carnal driven want, could drive a person insane.

Without conscious thought, Tess found herself on her back porch. Closing Buddy in the kitchen so he wouldn't bother her, want to sit on her lap and make her even warmer.

She sat and watched the darkened house next door. Was he simply lying there in the dark, too? Was he thinking about her? About wanting her? Probably not, he had other means of release she was sure. Women lived above the saloon for those kinds of things. Men had it easy, of course, easier than she did. Standing, she began the long walk to his back door. She didn't have to go in, possibly merely being closer to him would be enough.

"Did you need something, Doc? Someone in your house scare you?" Carter asked through the night as soon as he heard her soft step on his porch.

"No, just came over because I'm too damn hot," she said chuckling and stretched, the thin fabric of her nightgown clinging to her damp skin in places that made Carter's heart skip beats.

"I'm not sure you know what you're doing, Doc. I mean I'm not a strongly moral man, and, I can tell you, I'm having a hell of a time keeping my hands off you right now," he confessed from the darkness that was his home.

"That's the response I was hoping for, Sheriff. You said before you wanted me and now, I want you. Isn't that how these things usually work?" She was tantalizing him with possibilities that stood right in front of him as she took the last step that placed her within reach.

"They work a lot of different ways, but usually there's a little notice, a warming-up period so to speak," he told her. Unable to bring his hands up to put her from him, afraid to touch her in case it made him erupt into flames.

Tess rubbed her hands up his arms from his forearm over his biceps to his shoulders. She spent the time rubbing herself up against his arousal which he knew appeared, just as he told her, whenever she came near him.

Whispered words, "Are you sure you're not warm enough already?"

He grabbed her by the shoulders pulling her to him, his mouth covering hers, drinking from her as a man who had been denied succulence for too long.

"Stop me, stop me now, if you've changed your mind," he pleaded.

Tess hadn't changed her mind. She was thinking she had done the exact right thing tonight. She would have this to remember, to hold close to her heart when she returned to Michigan.

"I haven't changed my mind. I want this more than you know," she whispered between kisses and moaned, loud and long as he pushed aside the nightgown's neckline latching onto the eager nipple protruding there. He lowered them both to the couch and stretched out alongside her.

"Say my name, Tess. Say my name so I know you know who is giving you this pleasure, this passion," he begged as he took her lips again.

"Noah. Noah, Noah, Noah," she said breathlessly into his mouth, ending by plunging her tongue in along with the words, before Noah returned to suckle at her breasts. "This is, this feels amazing," Tess said, turning one nipple then the other to his seeking lips, not able to be content with his ministrations alone.

"If you like this, then you're really gonna like what I do next," he told her into her ear as he lowered his hand to slide up the length of her leg, unhindered to the soft curls at the top, then cupped her firmly. She felt the insertion of his finger, coaxing the hidden nub into presenting itself.

Another loud moan of pleasure and desire rewarded this action, her hips rotating in unison with his thumb as he pleasured her almost to completion. "Wait for me, Darlin'. I want to be in you when you reach your pleasure."

With that he brought his erection to her warm channel and slid in quickly. Tess felt the stinging of her tearing skin above all else and reacted, pulling away from him even though she thought she had been prepared.

"What the...?" Then it hit him, stopped him in mid-stroke, the knowledge that the woman he held in his arms had never been with a man physically.

"Don't stop, Noah. Please, I'm fine now. The pain just startled me...please?" Tess whispered into his ear, his head resting on her shoulder as he decided what to do.

Tess pushed her hips up to him, bringing him closer to her body then relaxed back to the cushion. Noah followed suit, not saying anything, but wanting to bring her back to the same height of desire and passion she had been at when he entered her so swiftly.

Soon her breaths were quickening and Noah was urging her to some sort of conclusion he knew her body didn't understand.

"Come on Darlin'. Let it go, don't hold back. Relax and feel me enter you, fill you, touch you as no one has ever done before." Leaning his mouth down he suckled on one breast, seemingly causing all sorts of physical responses deep inside Tess.

Her body pushed upward, trying to get closer to his, trying to keep him within her as she stiffened and he felt her muscles tighten around him. He felt a shudder and final release as she became pliable in his arms.

Noah held himself under tight control then withdrew, spending himself on her stomach between them, kissing her mouth again and cupping her breast to keep in contact with her. She held him tightly to her body as they calmed enough to breath normally.

Finally, Noah said, "Let me get you cleaned up. I didn't have any protection here, I don't usually...." He let the sentence die off. He didn't want Tess to think of him being with other women just as he was glad to learn she hadn't been with anyone else. Evidently, not even her husband.

"I can do that," she offered as he got some tepid water from the stove and wiped her stomach, washing his seed from her body.

He turned away to clean himself off. This isn't something he usually had to do. Self-pleasuring had passed by the time he was eighteen when his taste for more bi-partisan participation had developed.

Turning back, he found Tess had re-dressed herself in her nightgown. She had difficulty meeting his gaze, even in the pale moonlight. He stepped in front of her and asked, "Do you plan on leaving my fee on the table?"

She stared up at him then, trying to figure out what he said. As she must have realized what he meant she shook her head. "I'm sorry, Noah, I didn't mean it like that. It's just that I don't know what happens now."

"Now I watch to make sure you get home. I'd walk you but two people might be seen where as one small one might not be noticed. I'll stop by for coffee as usual and we can talk then if you want or we can admit we like one another and take it from there. Don't over think this, Tess." He steered her to his back porch before he stopped listening to reason and hauled her back into his bed like every muscle in his body was crying out for him to do.

CHAPTER TWELVE

Tess slept late, missing coffee time but as she felt the blood rush through her body, tried to figure out how she planned on facing him ever again. After what they had done, after she had shown herself to be a wanton, unable to control her baser needs. She buried her face into her pillow, but knew she would need to get up and dress for the day. Let Buddy out and handle any patients who showed up - and hide from her neighbor. Just a typical day. She could handle this.

But last night had been anything besides typical. Was it always like that? Was that what drove men and women to procreate? No wonder the human species was so prevalent on earth. How did she not know this? Not understood what the books meant?

Her toes curled remembering how her body responded to his. She seemed to vibrate with an over-whelming sense of euphoria before floating down from somewhere she went without realizing she had left her body.

She tried to take in all the sensations, all the ways her body enjoyed and reveled in this man's touch. But she found any words, any memories weak. She was unable to describe what she went through. It was an amazing ethereal experience that happened every day in people's lives.

Not hers. Not unless she could find a way to be with Noah again. If he was willing to be with her for as long as they had together. Before she must leave him and Forever.

The day pretty much went as Tess thought it would. A few simple doctor visitors, older people with not much else to do besides talk about their aches and pains. Not that Tess minded, especially today. It kept her mind off her neighbor who seemed to be taking up way too much of her waking time. It was bad enough to know he was going to front and center of her dreams from now on.

Tess was sitting on the sofa, a pile of yarn she thought to make into a scarf now that the mittens were finished for the children. She hadn't gotten very far, her mind going back to the night before, the night she humiliated herself with her neighbor, practically begging him to take her, offering herself up as if she was his to use however, he would.

She closed her eyes once again, hoping to forget how pitiful she sounded pleading with him. How humiliated she felt whenever she thought of facing him again.

When she opened them, Carter was standing in the dining room, the little dog quietly by his boots.

Tess jumped when she realized he was there watching her face, her emotions probably readable from across the room.

"I told you not to over think this, Doc." He walked silently towards her and sat next to her on the sofa. For a large man, it was surprising how easily he did it.

He took one of her hands unresistingly in his. "What's that supposed to be?" he asked looking at the wad of yarn sitting in her lap.

"It was supposed to be a winter neck scarf," she explained quietly, not peeking at him, not wanting to see what might be in his eyes.

"I never got to tell you how humbled I am that you chose me last night. If that's all we ever have together, I'll still count myself a lucky man." He paused as if expecting her to say something but she couldn't, not yet.

"I mean, I'm the sheriff. I'm here to protect you from men like me. You've got an ongoing criminal case I'm supposed to be solving, not taking you into my arms, holding you, caressing you, dreaming of you until I find myself looking over here all through the night. If you tell me that's all there will ever be, then I'll accept your decision. I won't like it, but I'll accept it." He spoke quietly as if someone else in the house might overhear them.

"But I was so brazen. Why did I do such a thing? I've never done anything like that before. It's like I was taken over by a power stronger than myself." She found she was still unable to look at him, just barely able to explain the desire that overtook her.

"And I'm glad you did. That you came to me since I haven't been able to come to you. You had to make the first step 'for all those reasons I just said. I was desperate for you, too." He seemed to hunt for words or expect her to tell him what she thought. He began speaking again, "You probably realized how drawn I was to you, how it was beginning to be a compulsion with me. I couldn't have held out too much longer so I'm glad you put us out of our misery. I care a lot about you and I want to be with you, all times of the day, not only to make love." His thumb rubbed small circles on her palm just as he had in another soft place the night before.

"Is that what it was? Did we make love?" she asked gazing into his eyes to see if she could discern the truth.

"That's what I thought it was. Don't you feel a connection, a need to be with one another that has nothing to do with having sex?" He asked her watching intensely as she absorbed the words.

"Is that love, then?"

"It seems to be the beginnings, for me, anyways. It started in earnest when you threatened to move away. I don't mind waiting while you get your degree, but I want you to come back to Forever when you're done. Come back for me. If there's another doctor here, then we'll find another small town that needs a doctor and a sheriff. There are plenty of new towns starting up all the time."

She smiled, liked his plans, knowing he'd wait for her, wanted her in his life forever in any town. "I hadn't thought about you waiting for me. It might be a long time."

"It doesn't matter as long as you agree to come back for me. I'd marry you before you left but you said they might not take a married woman so I kept my mouth closed. Hoped you'd realize what we have. I wouldn't have let you leave without telling you of my feelings. I was still holding out for another doctor to show up and for you to stay on here. I'm not a fool, Doc, I'd much rather have you stay."

"Why do you insist on calling me, Doc? I've told you, I'm not…." But she was interrupted with a kiss.

"Because I can't call you Darlin' in front of everyone," he said with a grin.

"Noah, I need to think about this." She felt him tense beside her so she looked at him quizzically.

"Sorry, Doc, you best not use my Christian name. It sends something through me that kinda gets things going," he admitted, leaning over to place his lips over hers again.

"Carter?" She looked for permission to continue and got it, "I need to think about this. I wasn't seeing my reactions for what they were. I thought it was simply lust. I never thought deeper about why I desired you when any other man never made me think, um-m-m, interesting thoughts."

"There's nothing simple about lust and I like you having interesting thoughts about me. Let me know when I interest you again, but for now, do we have an understanding between us? Can I continue with my plans, my dreams that you'll come back to me?" He seemed sincere and the knowledge warmed her heart.

"You have my promise." She accepted his kisses with a sigh.

He seemed content but still wanted to talk. "Can you explain about last night? I mean you are a widow, aren't you?"

"Yes, of course, only my husband was much older. I explained he was a contemporary of my father and he replaced my father in my life. He explained he wanted someone to help him reach his goals, not satisfy any long-forgotten need to procreate. I was very fond of him, grateful to him, but he was never a husband in traditional terms."

He nodded, accepting her explanation. He kissed her quickly on the lips before saying, "I better get home. I'll see you over coffee in the morning."

CHAPTER THIRTEEN

However, they didn't have coffee in the morning. A very worried husband showed up on Tess's front doorstep and practically wore a path in the foyer carpet waiting for Tess to dress before he drove her out to one of the small farms to deliver his first child.

"Let's go, Mr. Hatch," Tess said as she gathered her black bag.

"It's James, you can call me, James. I can't get used to being called by my father's name," he said as he helped her up onto the wagon seat.

Tess looked over at Carter's house and could see a lamp lit in the window. He knew she was leaving and he probably knew why. She should feel very lucky to have a man like that involved in her life. She let Buddy outside knowing Carter would make sure he got fed while she was gone. Perhaps between the two of them they could keep a pet.

When Tess got to the farm it was to find a scared young woman trying not to frighten her husband any more than he already was.

"Let's see how you're doing, Julia," Tess said lifting the bottom of the long-sleeved nightgown. "James, would you put on a large pot of water to a rolling boil for say five minutes then let it cool down without using any. Meanwhile make yourself a breakfast. It's going to be a long day no matter when this baby is born."

"I was afraid these were false labor and James went to get you for no reason. I mean, they just stopped. Then when I least expected, they began again only twice as strong. I was going to make jam from the berries I picked yesterday. I was fine, no warning or anything," the young woman said, needing to talk to express some of the energy building up inside her.

"That's the way it usually goes. Sometime the mother finds herself wanting to do extra things like clean cupboards or mop floors. I find the exercise actually is good and if you begin to slow down, I may have you walk around the room to get things going again," Tess explained as she checked Julia's abdomen and waited through another contraction as Julia held her breath.

"Remember what we discussed in the office, Julia? Don't hold your breath with a contraction. Breath through them. Otherwise you're cutting off oxygen to the baby, too." Tess peered about the room for the items she told Julia to have ready when the baby came.

"Sorry, it's just so natural to hold my breath. Is this going to get worse?" she asked worriedly.

"Every woman and birth is different, but yes, it's going to get worse than this. You'll find you will think your child was well worth it. I've delivered dozens of babies and you're doing very well," she praised the young mother-to-be knowing Julia would need all the encouragement she could get.

Tess wished she were in an operating theatre where it would be safe to use chloroform to ease the pain, but she didn't dare do so without an experienced assistant. Julia would have to give birth much the same as women had been doing for hundreds of years.

It was almost midnight by the time Tess presented James with his squalling son, washed clean and a healthy pink. Julia was presentable if worn-out. Tess left the new family alone to get acquainted. Pouring a cup of coffee for herself, she cut a slice of bread and spread it with butter. Since her patient couldn't eat, neither had Tess, only allowing a little clear broth for the mother during the long hours of labor.

Taking down the large washtub from the porch wall, Tess put the bloody sheets and cloths to soak in salt water. She looked at the larder and decided on meals for the next day. Without another woman in the house and Julia being a first-time mother, Tess planned on staying until James and Julia could handle having a family. She told James he could lie next to his wife so Tess eyed the short sofa as a resting place. Pulling a quilt off the back, she folded it for a pillow. It was still too hot to have more coverings on then necessary.

Tess heard the baby crying off and on through the night, but also heard both father and mother talking quietly to each other. Then the merciful quiet as the baby suckled and fell back to sleep. This was one reason Tess stayed with the infant and new mother. Questions came up, something she hadn't covered and then there was panic or worse.

Tess was up when James came out, a worried expression as he said, "I have to go and take care of the animals, but I don't want to leave Julia and little James."

"Go ahead. I'll go in and help Julia with her needs and you take care of what you need to do. Just keep your boots outside on the back porch and change into clean clothes after work before you hold the baby."

"Yes, Ma'am," he replied politely. "I appreciate all you did for my wife and son."

"It was a pleasure. I love bringing new life into the world," Tess told him honestly as she headed into the bedroom to help Julia begin her day.

After the third day, Tess announced to the couple, both sitting at the dinner table, "I'm very pleased with how well you two are doing. Take things slowly if you must, Julia. Don't bother dusting if you're too tired. Sleep when the baby sleeps, both of you, if you can, James. Make meals that are easy even if you must have stew or soup every night. I taught you some short cuts, James, so don't feel it has to be fancy, just nutritious. Julia will be able to help once she recovers some of her strength. The laundry is caught-up at the moment but that will change as soon as little James does what babies do. You'll both do fine, but I need to get back to town to be available to my other patients."

"I'll take you back, Ma'am, right after morning chores if that's all right?" James said.

"That should be fine. I'll start supper before I go and give Julia all my final instructions." Tess got up and washed the dishes as the new parents went to their room with their son.

James and Tess were halfway back to town when a buggy approached them at a pretty good clip, the driver immediately recognizable.

"Sheriff Carter," said Tess as they came even with one another. "Is there a problem? I was on my way back to my office just now."

"Your other expectant mother. She's in your place right now. I didn't know what else to do with her. I'll take you back with me, this buggy will be quicker than the wagon," he said as Tess was already getting down, her black bag in her hand.

"Thank-you again, Ma'am. I hope everything goes as well for this other mother," James called out as Carter turned the buggy and went quickly back towards town.

As they drove toward their destination, Tess asked, "Is there anything more you can tell me about my patient?"

"She didn't look good, pale but that could be her natural color, I guess. Her husband said her water broke and there was a lot of blood. He didn't seem to be comfortable talking to me, but was damn near scared out of his mind. None of it sounds good to me," he finished explaining what he knew.

"That's because none of that is good. She's not due for at least six weeks, possibly more, since she was a newlywed," Tess said worrying her lip with her top teeth.

"Could they have…. I mean could she be further along than that? You know began the honeymoon a little early?"

"Not that early. The baby would have been larger and I just saw her a couple of weeks ago. I see the mothers several times in the final trimester. She was doing fine when I last checked her." Tess went over all the possible outcomes in her mind of what she had been told and didn't like any of them.

Carter pulled up in front of the house. Tess jumped down with her bag, raced up the steps taking off her hat as she went. She found the couple in the little room off the examination room where they placed recuperating patients.

"Lillian, Mitchell, what seems to be going on? Are you in pain, Lillian?" Tess asked tying on a clean apron.

"She fainted or fell or something at home. I found her on the floor and there was bloody water everywhere. I picked her up and brought her here but you were gone," he said still unsettled by what had occurred.

"I've just delivered another baby and everything went fine so let's see how your little one is doing. Let me wash first then I'll take a look." Tess went to the kitchen to do just that.

Mitchell followed Tess out to the kitchen. "I can't lose her. I can't stand to think of losing her. If it's a choice between her or the baby, save my wife. We can have another baby, but if I lose my wife…I may as well be dead, too."

She could see he was tortured over his decision.

Coming out of the kitchen, Mitchell was on her heels as she said, "I hope it won't come to that. I'll try to save them both."

She looked up into the eyes of the sheriff who came back from dropping off the buggy and spoke of her fear and worry in a silent message.

"Stay here, Mitchell. I'll call you in after I've checked your wife." Tess said a silent blessing as Carter held out his arm to prevent Mitchell from following her.

She physically checked Lillian and as she did so the mother-to-be said, "If there's a choice between me and my baby, save my baby. I wouldn't want to live if it was at the cost of my child's life. Mitchell can find a new mother for our child. I've been happy with him and I can leave this world at peace."

Tess left the small room and said to Mitchell, a strong man, "I need you to carry Lillian to the examination room and place her on the table." Turning to Carter, she said quietly, "I need you to get Meredith's brother, and then get back here as soon as you can. I'm going to need an assistant and you're it."

Carter searched her face then nodded. "I'll be right back."

Between the two of them, Mitchell and Tess got Lillian undressed and lying on the table under an ironed sheet. Tess got out some of the equipment she would need while speaking to Lillian.

"I have performed this procedure many times. It sounds scary, but I assure you it is the only way to save both you and the baby."

Mitchell went over to Tess, grabbed her arm, and hissed, "I told you I don't care about the baby if there's a choice to make. I've made it."

Tess pulled her arm lose from his grip and said just as quietly, "This baby is over seven and a half months along and your wife's water is gone. She's having no signs of contractions. If the baby dies inside the womb, and she doesn't expel it on her own, it will turn gangrenous and kill your wife."

The dreaded disease, gangrene, reared its ugly head. Everyone knew someone who had died of gangrene in the war. The terrible weapon no one wanted to hear of took down hundreds of men on both sides and maimed many more. Mitchell blanched then nodded, letting Tess finish getting things ready.

Carter rushed back in. Tess told him to wash in the kitchen and put on the bibbed apron. Carter returned without his shirt having washed his entire upper body.

He was ready to help in any way Tess instructed him to do.

Reverend Jenkins entered the house unsure of what to expect, but Tess explained, "I'm closing the door now and I do not want to be disturbed." She saw the reverend hold Mitchell back and whisper in his ear as she closed the doors.

Turning to Lillian, Tess said softly, "It's time to put you to sleep for a little while. I promise to do my best."

"Carter, stand right there while I place this metal cage over Lillian's mouth and nose. You will have to hold it so the cloth doesn't touch her skin. See how I drop just a few drops of chloroform, don't saturate it. Now count for me Lillian, one, two, that's it," Tess said as if orchestrating a concert, everyone having a place to stand and job to do.

As she saw Lilian slumber, Tess expelled a deep sigh.

"Don't breathe in the fumes or you'll be on the floor next to her," she warned Carter. "I need you to be sure not to saturate the cloth, we have to keep her asleep so she won't feel the incision yet awake enough so that her heart won't stop," she explained to her now unwilling assistant as she wiped Dr. Lister's antiseptic over the protruding belly.

"Is the baby alive then? You're cutting it out?" Carter's eyes were wide but she saw no sense of doubt there.

"That's the only way to possibly save them. I'm hoping to get the infant out alive but it's immature. I need to make sure where it is. It isn't in the birth canal so I should be able to cut along here."

Taking the sharp scalpel, she made the incision following through with a long cut beginning at the navel and making a downward incision.

Carter winced but didn't hesitate to continue doing his job. Tess was also watching the drips, making sure he wasn't breathing in the strange solution.

She knew he watched as she made another cut. Reaching in, she pulled the baby out by its legs with one hand, swooping it up and out. She laid the infant on the now less sizable stomach searching for signs of life.

Tess cleared the baby's mouth with one finger and tapped his feet. Nothing.

Covering the baby's mouth with her own, she blew into the child, filling his lungs with air, then turned him over rubbing his back. Tess prayed and heard Carter pray along with her.

It seemed as if infinite time passed. There it was - a gurgle and a squall. A little person angry at whoever had disturbed his warm home where he had been content for months. Tess watched as the baby's skin went from a pale blue into a healthier pink.

Wiping the tears from her eyes with the back of her forearm, said, "And now for the mother."

The baby was placed to Lillian's side next to Carter who glanced down with an expression of awe.

Tess placed the after-birth and bloody-cloths in the slop bucket beneath the table. Taking a needle, she sewed furiously yet precisely while the infant continued to voice his displeasure at being cold, naked and in a bright light.

After being bent over the mother for several minutes, Tess stood straight instructing Carter, "You can stop the chloroform now, let her wake up. I'll take the baby and make sure he's all right." She smiled as she lifted the infant. "His lungs sound strong enough."

Carter seemed relieved at his loss of a job. He placed the cone and bottle on the movable table, corking the bottle to make sure it wouldn't affect Tess or the baby.

It wasn't long before the baby was swaddled tightly in a pillow case and was quietly watching what was going on in his new world. Lillian was groggy, but awake enough to know she had a son and they both seemed to be fine.

Mitchell finally opened the door. "I can't stand the wait, is she alive?"

"They are both alive. Lillian's just waking up now and will be tired. She'll need extra care as will your son."

At the movement of Lillian's head to try to see her husband, he stepped into the room and took her hand. "You're never to scare me like that again," he ordered her tenderly.

"I'll talk with you both later. Mitchell, would you like to hold your son, show him to his mother. I don't trust her to hold on to him until she's more awake, when we move her into the room next door," Tess said, covering the bucket and taking it with her.

Carter stepped out of the room. "I feel like I'm underdressed here, but before I go, I want to tell you how proud and amazed I am at what you can do." Then whispered, "And without a paper degree."

He reverted to his regular tone. "You got any more pregnant patients?" At Tess's shake of her head, he said, "Thank God. Sorry, Reverend." Then grabbing his shirt went out the back door.

Reverend Jenkins said a blessing over the new family and left for home. It was dark and he said that Meredith would be worried.

Mitchell stayed the night, trying to help his wife suckle and care for the infant. Tess was glad the baby had taken to the nipple and didn't seem to have trouble sucking although wasn't content with Lillian's milk at this time.

Tess would show them how to supplement the mother's milk in the morning or the infant would tire himself out too much working at getting too little. It was mostly due to the fact Lillian hadn't gone into labor. Tess didn't want the young mother to think she couldn't feed her son, but it might take longer for her milk to come in.

CHAPTER FOURTEEN

Mitchell left in the morning without breakfast, but returned three hours later with luggage, a cradle and his mother-in-law who swooped down on the two patients. She admonished her son-in-law over and over for not stopping and picking her up when he brought his wife in, but Mitchell didn't pay too much attention to her. He told Tess, later, he knew his mother-in-law was the best caregiver for Lillian so he would put up with a lot of orders and reprimands.

Tess fixed the meals but otherwise wasn't inconvenienced by the little family in the side room. After all, that was what Robert said it was there for. It was funny, but her thinking of Robert must have conjured him up, in a small way.

There was a rapping at the front door and Tess opened the door to Abe, the little dog barking furiously until Tess admonished him by saying, "Friend, Buddy."

"I thought you'd want this letter since it's from Doctor Waverly," the thin, pleasant young man said indicating the envelope on top of the box he held in his hands. "The doctor told me to bring any packages over in case it was something he needed so I brought this one. Should I put it on the desk like always, Mrs. McLeish?"

"That will be fine, Abe. You're familiar with the house then?" she asked following him to the room.

"I stayed here during the influenza last year. I didn't have anyone at home so Doctor Waverly took me in. I owe him my life, I suppose." He walked back to the front door. "Then you gave me this neat little scar, well, rather you sewed me up real neat like." He bent his elbow to indicate where the scar was.

"I remember you were an excellent patient," she teased him and watched as his face blushed with pride.

Tess handed him a coin and he tipped his cap. "Thank you, Ma'am."

Tess wished she could invite Carter over for supper, but there were already three extras for meals and even their usual morning coffee had been eliminated with so many watchful eyes. If everything went well, Mitchell and his family would soon go home, taking mama-in-law with them.

It was two more days before Tess was satisfied that Lillian and her son were well enough for the short buggy ride to their ranch. After a stir in the morning, the patients went home where Tess would visit Lilian to make sure everything was healing correctly.

Tess took Mitchell aside to make sure he understood Lillian should not conceive for at least a year and it would be up to him to ensure that. She gave him a few of the condoms she found in the cabinet in the examination room that Robert must have kept on hand for similar purposes. Red faced, he assured Tess he would protect Lillian from going through this again so soon.

Tess was excited. She was free to invite Carter over for supper and possibly more. She wasn't sure what she had in mind, but was sure he could help with the decision. However, Carter didn't walk the path between their homes that night nor did he come with his empty coffee cup held out in the morning.

Tired of not knowing what was going on, Tess placed her best-looking hat on her head and went to the grocer's where she was sure to be told all the news and gossip without ever asking.

Dorothy, the grocer's wife and best baker in town, tallied up the cost of the goods in Tess's basket and relayed news of the past week, excluding the new babies since Tess was already well aware of those events.

"And there was that to-do in the saloon. Not that I have firsthand knowledge or anything," she said. Tess silently thought - it didn't keep you from telling me about all the other things. Then thought she was being uncharitable since the only reason Tess was there was to hear the gossip.

Tess asked, looking over the tomatoes for a second time, "To-do at the saloon, you say?"

"Yes, but the sheriff was already there. Theo, the bartender, said the sheriff's been buying Goodyear's, you know, rubbers. We both know why he would need those." She raised her eyebrows and continued, "I mean, I know he's not a married man and all, but he should be held to higher standards than consorting with a cheap saloon girl."

"Like an expensive one?" Tess asked knowing her sarcasm would go unnoticed, but thinking about Carter's purchase of protection. Were they for himself or for her or did he buy them on a regular basis?

Dorothy stopped tallying and looked at Tess to see if she were seriously asking then continued because, evidently, this little piece of gossip had been held for last for a reason. "He, Sheriff Carter that is, broke-up a fight between that red-head and some man who said he was her husband and wanted her to come home. Why any man would want a wife back that had been doing what she was doing is beyond me. You'd think he would have been glad to be rid of her, but it didn't seem that way."

"No, you wouldn't," Tess answered not knowing how to agree with the woman to keep her talking. "But, now what did Sheriff Carter, do?" asked Tess as if just slightly curious.

"Oh, he poured a bucket of water over the both of them. You could hear the shrieks clear across the street, from the red-head, I suspect. Not the husband, he was just cussing a blue-streak. Not that I heard all of this, of course. I wouldn't stoop so low as to listen to someone else's marriage woes." Dorothy wrapped the piece of bacon Tess had asked for and added it to the tally.

Tess kept from gritting her teeth and said smiling, "And Sheriff Carter's part in all this other than the bucket of water…?"

"He tied their hands together. I mean, to one another, and tossed them into the back of a wagon. Told Andrew at the livery he was taking them home where they belonged and would be back in a couple of days with the wagon. That'll be two dollars and fourteen cents," Dorothy said, seemingly very pleased with her sale.

"Thank you, so much." Tess paid the money. Glad she now knew where Carter had disappeared to. Although the part about his being in the saloon and, probably daily, didn't sit as well as she liked.

Susan Payne

On the way home, Tess diverted her path to the rectory to talk with Meredith. Anything to take her mind off Carter and his buying items best left unmentioned.

Meredith was home and invited Tess in for tea. "Come in, I've been needing to speak with you but you've been so busy. I heard you actually breathed life into Lillian's son. That he would have died without you knowing what to do."

"I see Dorothy's been busy. Must have pumped the mother-in-law for information. I only let Lillian know what happened while she was under sedation. I was more worried the baby was not developed enough to breathe on his own. Early babies have immature lungs. I think Mathew will be just fine as he grows. But this is not what you seemed so excited to tell me about." Tess watched her friend closely.

"No, it's to tell you I decided to do as you suggested and invite a man, I was interested in, to Sunday dinner. I invited, Andrew, the gentleman who works for Weber & Weber's Coach Line. He takes care of the horses and maintains the harnesses," Meredith said proudly.

"Oh, I know him. He's always so nice and never complains about the odd times I need a buggy."

"Yes, he is very nice. Although he said he enjoyed the dinner and thanked me profusely, he hasn't come back. I mean, he said good morning when we ran into each other at church but that's all. It's not like I have any reason to go to the livery. Do you have any more good ideas for me?" Meredith asked, almost pleading.

"Ask him to dinner again and when you do, ask if he would mind sitting with you during the service. Then

124

he can walk you home easier while the Reverend is finishing saying goodbye to the congregation. Just stay outside on the porch until your brother gets home."

"That may work. Then we'd have a little time alone to talk. I really like him, Tess, but I'm not sure he feels the same way," Meredith confided, her self-confidence at the lowest Tess had ever seen it.

"He's not a fool. If he likes women, he will finely realize you like him and he will be flattered. Then he will find a way to see more of you. Even if it's simply sitting on your porch with you," Tess prophesied.

"Do you really think so?" Meredith was smiling shyly and looking years younger.

"I really think so." Tess promised herself to talk with the stupid man if he does anything else.

CHAPTER FIFTEEN

It was as she washed her personals that Tess was again reminded someone was still obsessed with her. She realized one of her camisoles was missing. She only owned three, which she rotated, always having at least one clean one. She was sure she put it with the other things to be washed and now it wasn't there. The clothesbasket sat on the back porch so the intruder might not have gotten into the house. Could have come by while she was shopping or visiting Meredith. Tess hadn't realized having Lillian and her mother there might have been beneficial to her, too. She will have to be more watchful again after getting lax about her safety these past several days.

Tess was standing at her sink when she saw Carter, a few days growth of beard on his face, and she impulsively went onto the porch and greeted him with a wide smile.

"Hello, Doc. Miss me?" he asked cheekily, knowing she was devouring him with her eyes.

"I did miss you, Carter. I hear you're living up to your name of peacekeeper. Perhaps other couples will hire you to smooth out their marital problems," she told him, wanting to step off the porch and throw herself at him.

"So, the gossip mill didn't stop while I was away. Give a man hope for the generations to come. Speaking of which, Mitchell's family doing all right? No problems creep up?" Buddy jumped around trying to get his attention which he finally did as Carter squatted and rubbed the dog's ears.

"I sent everyone home and it's been so quiet around here I can hear my own breathing," she said teasingly.

"I'll have to take your word for that." Carter felt his groin tighten and his heart beats speed-up with thoughts of what he wanted to do with this woman so enticingly standing there in welcome. His gaze searched for signs of passion or that she had missed him as much as he had missed her. See if there was still desire between them.

"Are you hungry? I can make you something quick."

Words he was happy to hear. Knowing she wasn't regretting their time together. Wishing he could say otherwise, he answered, "I'm fine, thanks. Need to clean up. I was on the road longer than I thought I'd be. Some people don't know when they got it good." Rubbing the back of his neck, he realized he needed a haircut.

Forcing his feet to continue to his back porch, he wanted to turn and take her into his arms. Nuzzle into the warm smell of her and hug her body to him for days. He missed her, too much. More than he would have expected after a few day's trip.

He had listened to the couple he was delivering home argue and cuss at each other before finally talking and listening to one another. Followed by them practically making love in the back of the wagon before he got them all the way to their farm.

Everything reminded him of Tess. How they were past the arguing and fighting stage and could get right to the loving. That is if she wanted to. He must leave it up to her. It would be her reputation, her standing in the town as a medical professional in jeopardy. Her ability to attend college that would be impacted if they were ever discovered to be more than neighbors.

He knocked the mud off his boots before stepping onto the porch and thought, I really need this bath and I need it to be a cold one.

Tess had turned away before she invited Carter to her bed, invited him to make love with her again. She needed to get control of herself, evidently just as he had. If he could speak with her in a normal manner, then she could do so as well.

It was dark, but Tess could see Carter remove the last of his clothes and step into the bathtub he'd been preparing for the last half hour. Tess licked her lips, her mouth dry from desire for this man who hadn't done anything to attract her attention. Well, he'd done nothing except strip naked on his back porch silhouetted by the oil lamp on the floor behind him. Tess held her arms across her breasts which had been tingling ever since she sat down quietly in the chair to watch - simply to watch.

After several minutes, Carter stood up and dried himself with the small towel, letting his erection show dominate in the light from the lamp. Then he walked into the house after taking one long look over to the porch as if he could see her in the darkness.

That was an invitation and if it wasn't, Tess was going to accept it as one.

By the time Tess finally found the courage to walk over to this man's house in her nightclothes again, he was dressed in his trousers and nothing else. Sitting with his bare foot braced on the chair rail, he set his empty bowl down and smiled a wide grin in welcome.

"I was hoping you were going to come over and put me out of my misery. I haven't had a coherent thought since the last time we were together here. I can't sit on that couch without remembering how you felt in my arms, under me or hear your little pants and those moans that drove me crazy. Those moans haunt my nights, Darlin'."

He stopped when he saw her face and his brows drew down in concern. "You're not here to stay? To make love?"

"Yes, I came because I couldn't stop thinking about us. What we did and how good it felt," she admitted as he came closer and pulled her into his arms.

"Am I rushing you?" he asked then covered her mouth with his, his hands covering her breast over the gown and wrapper, the only things she wore to bed. "I do want it to be your decision, but you can't blame me for trying to make it as difficult for you as possible to turn me away."

"Not really but I'm not sure what my part is in all of this. Last time it seemed like you did the work and I simply enjoyed it all."

"That is your part. I get to kiss and lick and suck everywhere, anywhere and you just lay back and enjoy it." His words were separated as he put actions to words, pulling her wrapper off and getting his hands under her gown to lift it from her body.

She pleaded, "Noah, I need to touch you, too. To feel you with my hands, my mouth."

"Alright, I'd like that too, believe me. Come here and you can have your way with me."

He led her to his room. Noah lay on the bed, his belt and trousers still in place as Tess kneeled next to him, smoothing her fingers and hands over his chest covered with dark curling hairs. Rubbing her cheek against his chest, she stopped to listen to the wild beating of his heart. She licked his nipples dragging her tongue across his chest from one to the other. She practically purred with pleasure that she could bring this huge male to lie passively awaiting her touch in trembling anticipation.

Tess continued to stroke his shoulders and down his muscled arms to his forearms. Forearms strong enough to hold his weight off her while they made love, while he lowered himself into her and then back up. Her hands caressed from his shoulders to his stomach.

She put her hands on his belt and unbuckled it, pulling it free so she could get to the buttons on his trousers.

Noah grabbed her hands saying, "I don't think I can stand to have you touch me right now. I'm not going to last through this if you continue. Let me take over."

Tess lay to his side, making herself available to his eyes, his hands, his mouth. Noah covered her mouth with his. Letting his tongue slide in and out as he teased her nipples between his finger and thumb. He was rewarded with her moan of desire. Those moans encouraged him to cover the peaks with his mouth, first one than the other as his hand moved down to between her legs.

The moan of appreciation was offered to Noah's pleasure and soon he was reaching toward the little packet he bought at the saloon. Tearing it open with his teeth, he slid it on before gratefully entering Tess as she waited less than patiently for him to join with her.

"Oh, Noah, this is even better than before. I didn't remember it being this good," she told him encouragingly as he made the long strong strokes that she seemed to appreciate the most.

Despite Noah's plans to make this session last into the night, it was complete for both of them in too short a time. "I'm sorry, Tess. I was afraid I wasn't going to hold back for very long. I was too hungry for you." He spoke quietly to her, staying away from words he thought would make her run from him and never come back.

He was still trying to catch his breath when he smiled remembering the anticipation of getting his belly scratched as she had Buddy. This was so much more than he ever dreamed possible. He pulled her close. Thankful to have her in his bed.

Tess, catching her breath from her earth-shattering orgasm, said, "Noah, I felt like I died and woke up in your arms. You have nothing to apologize for, believe me."

Noah kissed her mouth leisurely. "You're good for a man's confidence. I felt the earth move somewhere along there, too. It just seems like a big work up for a very short finale."

"Isn't that what it always is?"

He answered earnestly cradling her body to his.

"They're always different yet the same, I guess, but with you there's more. I don't know how to explain. I enjoy being with you so much I can't seem to get enough of you. I hope that's what you feel, too, then I won't have to worry about you leaving me."

Tess moved to snuggle to his side, enjoying the afterglow of their lovemaking and facing the fact she should probably go back to her own house.

Noah moved off the bed, taking care of the protection he wore when entering her. Tess was thankful for his consideration. She couldn't be with child while finishing her classes. She hated to think what the professors and other students would think about an un-wed mother getting a doctorate. It wouldn't be allowed, she was sure.

Returning to bed, he pulled her close again. He kissed the top of her head as if he enjoyed being able to hold her while letting his thumb rub against her skin. Tess wanted to lie there, enjoying this closeness to Noah, yet knew it was a bad idea to get too close to him. She was going to have to leave Forever at some point. Becoming too attached to this man could tear her and all her plans asunder.

Tess was thinking about their lovemaking when she heard the soft even snores of Noah taking his reward for pleasuring her. His body was relaxed and revitalizing itself. Tess new that physically he needed to rest before making love again yet felt driven to touch him, caress him in the same ways he caressed her.

She loved the texture of his chest, the play of muscles under her fingers - then she dared move lower. She knew the mechanics, the medical explanation for his reaction to her touch but she marveled at the smoothness, the velvety softness and the underlying strength of the engorged shaft. She was so enthralled with his member she was un-aware Noah was watching her face as she touched him, worshiped him until she glanced up.

"Do you know what you're doing, Tess? I have trouble keeping my hands off you, even right after making love, too. We may have begun something we'll soon lose control of. I want you again and I think you desire me, but should we allow ourselves to continue to the normal finish so soon again tonight?"

She stroked his erection, petting it gently as she spoke. "Why not take what we can while we can. You're in a dangerous job and I have a deranged man stalking me. Perhaps we should be doing this rather than our mundane day jobs."

"Maybe you're right. I shouldn't hold back from what I've wanted to do to you. Live for the now, not for the what now."

Rolling over he took Tess with him, pinning her to the bed with his leg and arms. He kissed her breast, but didn't stay there long, lowering himself and sliding between her legs, letting his mouth eagerly cover her core. His tongue slid in and she felt her response to its touch.

Tess didn't know what to do as her passion rose. She pulled his head to her but then pleaded, "I need to touch you, Noah. I need to pleasure you."

Noah pulled himself level with her. "This pleasures me just fine. It's new for me, but, if you want, I'll make you in charge. I'll help you take my role."

He placed Tess over his manhood, setting her on his thighs as he put another rubber on. Then helped Tess lower herself onto his hard shaft.

She moved tentatively, unsure of what would hurt his sensitive body part. "Don't worry, Tess, I don't think you could hurt me right now if you tried."

He put a hand on each side of her waist and guided her as she rode him. Her breathing increased followed by the low moans. She leaned forward and he placed his hand at the nub as she rocked on his hand as well as his erection.

The second climax was a little slower in coming, but was just as rewarding as the first. Tess liked being able to control her own pleasure, but enjoyed being able to watch Noah's reaction to what she was doing to him, with him, more.

She smiled as she lay on his chest, hearing his heartbeats return to normal, knowing she was responsible for his pleasure this time.

He spoke and she heard the rumble through his chest. "I liked to watch you as we made love. I was so enthralled watching you I almost forgot my part." He chuckled as she gave him an unbelieving expression. "I said almost."

"I think I should go back home. I woke you up once already and feel guilty because I know you're tired. I think I'm satiated now. Perhaps this will hold me over till tomorrow night."

Carter groaned and rolled onto his belly, hiding his private parts too late.

Tess leaned down and kissed his lips as he turned to tell her goodnight. Bending over, she picked up her gown and wrapper and quickly re-dressed.

CHAPTER SIXTEEN

Tess missed Buddy's usual greeting at the kitchen door. She thought he must be tired out from chasing ground-squirrels that tease him unmercifully during the day while gathering their winter store of food. Tess lit the small lamp in the kitchen and carried it upstairs.

As the shadows disappeared in the lamp's light, Tess heard Buddy whining. Straining her eyes trying to see why the dog would be in distress in the empty hallway, her light hit and lingered on the shape of a man kneeling, holding the furry little dog by the neck.

"Abe? What are you doing up here? Let go of Buddy!" Tess said sternly.

"I think he'll stay right here until you come up to talk with me. I know where you've been and you wouldn't want that to get all over town now would you?" His tone threatened everything Tess held dear. Carter, Buddy and her reputation.

Continuing to climb, she hoped Abe would understand her independence and leave before things became worse. "What I do is my own business. No one owns me and I am free to see anyone when I like."

He grabbed Tess's arm when she reached the top of the stairs and pushed her into her room. The bed was already turned down for the night as she left it. She went to the corner where the chair was, taking away the more intimate bed from Abe's view.

Tess heard the door to Robert's room snap close then Buddy scratching and whining. Before she could see what had happened, Abe came in with the lamp, acting agitated. He paced back and forth, muttering, arguing with himself. Buddy continued a non-stop digging at the bottom of the door.

Abe, now holding a knife in his hand, said angrily, "Why would you do this to me? Why would you go to him when you knew I'd be waiting for you? I was here to protect you, to take care of you. I promised that when I saw you crying for that damn Doctor Waverly. He left you after bringing you here, without giving you a chance. Well, I've given you more than one chance. Now, I'm disgusted to find you coming home to me after being with him. Smelling of him."

Tess sat in the chair in her room, sorry she hadn't decided to stay the night with Noah. But that was useless wishing. She had to try to get Abe calmed down and perhaps she could talk some reason into him.

"Abe, I'm very sorry. I didn't realize I was making you wait." She tried to sound conciliatory as her mind raced to figure out how to escape.

"Don't lie to me, you're just too selfish. You were doing what you wanted to, regardless of my feelings." He slammed his fist into his own chest.

Still trying to reach the young man she knew or thought she knew, she spoke quietly. "I'm sorry, Abe. How can I make it up to you?"

Abe stopped his erratic pacing then turned towards her. "I will have to think on that. I am disappointed, of course, but maybe we can still make this work."

"You're right, Abe, that sounds like what we should do." Tess hoped agreeing was the way of getting him to calm and become rational again.

"What are we having for supper? What are you making me for supper?" he asked out of the blue.

"Are you hungry? Would you like me to make you supper?" Tess responded thinking she would have more of a chance to run if they were in the kitchen. More of a chance to signal Carter she needed help.

"No, not now. I've already ate supper," he snapped at her.

"I'm sorry, I forgot. Did you want me to fix something special for tomorrow?"

She was hoping Noah would stop by for coffee and notice something strange in the morning. She would need to keep Abe from doing anything to her till then and making plans for supper seemed like a good start.

"No, we'll have to leave now. You and the sheriff have ruined everything." Then he thumped his chest with the hand that held the knife saying, "Can't you make that damn dog shut-up? I can't think and I have to change my plans. Get rid of the sheriff. We can't stay here anymore."

Buddy stopped whining and scratching at the door but was now barking and making a commotion trying to get out of the bedroom.

"I can speak with the sheriff. Explain I didn't understand what you wanted but now I do," Tess said hoping this would keep Abe from sneaking next door and killing Noah while he slept.

"He won't leave you be now that he's got a taste of you. I'll figure out what to do with him later." He looked decisive for the first time that night. "Get over here. We're going over to the livery and take one of the buggies. I've got a place where no one will find you."

"Shouldn't I dress? I can't go out in my bedclothes." Tess tried to prolong the time until she would be in his control completely. While she was in her home, she still felt she held some power.

"No, it won't matter. No one but me is going to see you." He grabbed the top of her arm and began to pull a reluctant Tess with his free hand, the knife still held menacingly in the other.

As they began down the dark staircase, someone dove out of the darkness into them both. Abe waved the knife and blood dripped quickly onto the stairs making them slippery as Tess gasped in pain. Covering her forearm with her other hand to stem the flow, she stumbled down the steps.

Noah stopped to help her as soon as he realized she was injured.

"I'm fine. I can handle this wound. Stop Abe. He's gone mad and has a knife."

That command had Noah taking the stairs two at a time, trying to catch the young man who had a head-start and knew how to disappear in the town.

Tess let a frantic Buddy out of the room. He leapt and ran around and around her feet as she tried to get downstairs to see to her injury. Pulling up the bottom of her wrapper, she held it tightly over the cut. It was soaked with blood quickly so knew she needed to get downstairs before she lost much more and passed out.

Once in the examination room, she lit one of the lamps and looked at the gash. It would mend, she thought as she applied a bandage tightly to her own arm, having trouble securing the end since she could only use one hand to tie it off. She took one end of the cloth into her mouth and made a decently neat knot.

Afraid she would be a distraction to Noah and a target for Abe if she went out into the house or lit more lamps, she remained in the room. Buddy stayed by her side when suddenly, he raced towards the kitchen yipping. Tess could hear him scratching at the back door to be let out.

Tess went through the dark house, thinking no one would see her if she didn't light the lamps. When she slid into the kitchen quietly, she heard the deep moan through the door. Tess looked out the window to see Noah, wearing only his trousers sprawled across the porch, his hand barely reaching the bottom of the door.

Opening the door, Buddy rushed through, sniffing and licking Noah as Tess dropped to her knees to help with his injuries. Blood encrusted his hair as she checked his head finding a long cut through his hairline.

"Noah, Noah! Try to answer me. I have to get you up to see if you're hurt anywhere else."

The semi-conscious man made another moan but seemed to have understood her because he moved his legs, getting his knees under him. With her help he stood, his head lowered but he was standing.

She knew she couldn't brace his entire weight on her own. "Can you walk a little? Possibly inside to the table?"

"Hmmm." Was his only reply but he shuffled his feet. Tess opened the door supporting him as she guided him into the dark kitchen. They found their way to the chair by the table and he collapsed onto it.

"Sit here, can you do that while I light the lamp?" Tess asked unsure he could stay upright without her beside him. At his nod, she quickly went to find a lamp.

Once the lamp was lit, she sat it on the kitchen table to examine the wound on Noah's temple and then his eyes. She looked over his body for any other signs of injury and asked, "Can you make it to the examination room? I'm going to need to stitch this up and watch you closely for at least twenty-four hours. You have a concussion."

He staggered to his feet but remained upright. "I think the S.O.B. hit me with a piece of wood for the stove, fresh off the pile," he said with humor. "I cut it myself before I left town."

"How did you know Abe was in here?" she asked as she looked over his head wound.

"Buddy. I saw your lamp fade as you went upstairs. It went out so I thought you closed your door, but then a little while later I saw Buddy jumping up higher than the window sill and he tore down the curtains."

He winced as she wiped the blood away to better see the wound. "I knew you wouldn't have let him do that so I came over to investigate. Caught some of what you and Abe were saying. I just wasn't sure how to grab him without getting you hurt." His gaze went to her bandaged arm. "I guess I didn't. I'm sorry."

"I'm not any better. I told you to go after him and he clonked you on the head." She was just as regretful.

"Yeah, and I thought he would have kept running. Instead, he waited for me right outside the door and gave me a good reminder to look before I leap."

After lighting more lamps, Tess cleaned out several splinters from his scalp then placed several of her neat sutures so the cut didn't even show.

"Now I want you to try to rest in the room next door. I'll wake you every hour or so to make sure you're not in a coma."

"Like hell, I will. I'm going to get that little, er, Abe, and make sure he knows never to bother you again. Hell, Doc, he cut you," Noah said getting agitated. "I don't want to think what he could have done to you. I should have known it was him."

"No one could have known." She finished dabbing salve on the stitches. "You are not leaving and you are certainly not going to get on a horse and try to find Abe right now. He's only a danger to me and you'll be with me all night."

"I wasn't planning on leaving you alone, Doc. I could call some help in."

"Go and lay down. I have to sew this cut closed then I'll come in to check on you. I plan on sleeping in the other bed so leave me the soft one," she said teasingly.

Noah focused on the arm wrapped with the blood-stained bandage. "You can't mean to sew your own arm, Honey. Not after all you've been through." His brows drew down in worry.

"I'm the only one able to do it. I have a steady hand and thank God, it's my left arm. If you're not going to rest, at least don't say anything to me while I do this. It's not something I do every day and I'm not used to being one handed while I'm doing it." She rethreaded a clean needle with silk thread and began unwinding the saturated cloth.

"I can help, just tell me what to do," he said with determination.

"Alright, three hands may be better than one. Hold these forceps like this to hold the skin together then I can suture better. I'll simply use continuous rather than individual ones that would require me to tie each one off." She winced as she placed the needle through her own skin on the first of many sutures.

An hour later, Noah was lying on his cot and Tess was laying on hers when out of the dark Noah's voice said, "I thought we might be sleeping together tonight, but this isn't what I had in mind."

"You have a concussion. This is as close as you're going to get to sleeping with me. Now close your eyes and take advantage of the sixty or so minutes I'm going to give you before I check on you again." She spoke in a no-nonsense tone.

Noah did so and fell immediately to sleep. Buddy was sleeping in front of the closed door and would warn them if anyone tried to enter. Tess looked up at the ceiling and wondered if there would be a way of saving Abe. If as a doctor, she could find a way the man wouldn't be locked away in an institution for the mentally insane. She would need to think of someone who could help her, perhaps someone her husband or father knew.

After waking up every half hour or so all night, making sure Noah was fine, Tess over-slept. Once the sun was up, she woke to find Buddy at the foot of her bed and the other one empty.

Pulling her tangled nightgown from around her legs, she said, "Buddy, he better be coming back from the privy when I get out there or there's going to be hell to pay." Finally, freed of the long gown, she went to see if Noah was indeed in the back yard.

There was no sign of Noah. Tess hurried upstairs, stepping over the dried blood on the wood steps and continued to her room to dress for the day. She would look for Noah in his usual haunts and if she didn't find him, she'd check at the livery to see if he took his horse.

She was coming downstairs when she saw Noah, dressed in his usual sheriff's clothing on the path between their houses. She headed to the kitchen in time to have him reaching for the locked door with a key in his hand.

"Did you take my key?" she asked, diverted from her original chastisement.

"No, Robert gave me a key years ago. When he moved in, he thought I should have it in case I needed to retrieve anything while he was out with a patient. He didn't start leaving his front door unlocked until a year or so ago. By then, he realized no one was going to tamper with his things." Noah put the key into his pocket.

"Well, you're supposed to be in bed," she said emphatically and watched as desire deepened the color of his eyes. "Oh, for pity sakes, Noah. I told you that you have a concussion which means you need to rest - no stimulants, no lovemaking."

"And I told you not to call me, Noah, in that breathless tone or my thoughts go directly to the bedroom – and you leaning over me doing all the work." A grin appeared across his stubble covered face.

"I didn't and it wouldn't matter because you won't listen to me as a doctor," she told him getting the fire stirred to life in the stove.

"I'm sorry. I know you want what's good for me but I had to see if Abe would be crazy enough to go into work this morning like nothing happened." At Tess's raised eyebrows in question, finished with, "He's not. He didn't go back to Mrs. Whites either or at least not for long. Most of his clothes are gone and it looks as if he packed in a hurry. Maybe even last night before he came here." He shook his head. "I should have gone after him."

"He hit you too hard. I don't know how long you were out there unconscious but probably long enough for him to pack and leave." She began slicing bread to fry.

"You're probably right. Andrew, at the livery, said one of the stage horses was gone this morning. Abe must have taken it. I told him to contact his employer and let them know Abe is a fugitive. For them to let the local law know if Abe shows up for his back pay."

He took the cups down for coffee and placed them on the table. "Andrew will take over the ticket office, too. Checked the box room and didn't notice anything missing. I told Andrew to tell anyone interested that Abe is wanted in connection with mail tampering. That way, they'll know he's a fugitive and won't help him if he stays around here. I'll send flyers out as soon as I'm given the all clear by my doctor to ride." He said cheekily, "I told Dorothy."

"Here, eat your breakfast. No coffee, it's a stimulant," she said, filling the cup with water then placed his plate in front of him.

"How's your arm?" he asked as he swiveled in his chair to face the table to eat.

"I have more sympathy with my patients now," she said as she sat down.

"You've always had sympathy for your patients, Doc. This will just make you more so, I suspect. Probably make you mother them all, no matter what their age." He slid the last of the fried eggs into his mouth. "Coffee would really taste good right about now."

"No stimulants," she repeated. At the look he was throwing her way she said more quietly, "And no lovemaking."

To her surprise, Noah stayed at her house the whole day. Not getting in her way as she went about seeing a few patients with minor ailments and explaining how she scratched her arm while cleaning-out the old chicken pen in the back yard. No one questioned her about the story. Noah stayed out of sight until the patients were gone then showed up by Tess's side.

"Will you take this letter over to Andrew so it will go out on the next stage? I wrote to a colleague, an alienist, at the hospital Doctor McLeish and I worked out of in Chicago. He specialized in diseases of the brain and other irregularities of the mind. I want his opinion on Abe and perhaps he can give us some insight as to what Abe might do in the future."

"I'll take it over now but I plan on having Abe in custody long before you get an answer back from this doctor." Noah took the envelope from her, waving it in the air before leaving.

CHAPTER SEVENTEEN

That didn't happen. Abe seemed to have disappeared off the face of the earth. He didn't really have any friends but seemed friendly to everyone. Many people didn't even know his last name. He was simply the nice young man who ran the ticket office. No one sent for any of the items left in Abe's room so Mrs. White boxed them up and stored them in the attic in case he returned for them. All this Tess learned as she tried to find out more about the man, she wished she had been able to help.

"

Tess knew Noah was anxious for the stage to arrive. H was waiting for any information from local lawmen could contact him quickly when Abe showed up in their town. The two of them spoke about the difficulty of finding Abe, especially if he moved around. Part of the problem was that Abe didn't appear to be dangerous. He never flaunted rules or laws, didn't drink or fight. He wasn't going to come into most lawmen's line of sight. Not a man they should worry about being in their towns.

"Doc, I got flagged down by Andrew. Gave me a couple of letters for you. One is from that fancy head-doctor in Chicago, I think," Noah called out as he came up the back steps to get ready for dinner. Tess placed a pitcher and bowl on a washstand outside and kept a clean towel handy there for his use. Noah changed from washing-up on his porch to washing-up on hers.

"Supper's almost ready. One of your favorites, chicken livers and onions," she said taking the letters and slitting Robert's open first.

"You always cook them up perfectly. Breaded and fried crispy yet still moist."

Tess smiled at the compliment knowing Noah ate just about anything put in front of him except broccoli.

"Well, Robert's married to Millicent. That's no surprise after all this time in St. Louis. They plan on moving into their own home." As she scanned the page, she supplied, "He hasn't found a doctor to take over here so will appreciate it if I would pack everything up for him and send it. He says he'll pay me for my time doing so."

She snapped the paper in the air in frustration. "He truly is the most thoughtless person I have ever met. Does he think I was merely here to watch over his possessions until he orders me to pack them and send them on? I should write back and tell him to come and get them himself," she said angrily.

"Come on, Doc. Cool down and sit here. Have some of this wonderful looking lemonade. Mm-m-m, doesn't it just look delicious?" He poured some into the glass in front of her.

Tess laughed at her own bad humor and his good one. "I know, I shouldn't have expected anything more from Robert. He did offer to sell me the items before, but without a degree, I can't really be in practice. I've stepped over the boundaries a few times already."

"Let's eat the nice meal you cooked us and we'll read the letters afterwards. I don't like to see you upset like this. We can get married and to hell with the rest of it," he said simply, spooning the crispy coated pieces of liver onto his plate then hers.

"I'm sorry. You are right. I can't change anything this late." She sat down at the table with ill grace and ate his most favorite meal and her least.

After the dishes were done, which Noah always helped with, the couple went into the parlor so Tess could read the thick letter from the Chicago doctor. "Oh, this is interesting. This doctor says he has had several cases similar to what I wrote him about. I didn't say it was me who was involved, merely a patient." She perused the next paragraph and read aloud, *"The subject of the patient's interest is often followed, even during routine daily activities. There are often personal items collected by the patient. The more personal the better in their demented state even to include the cutting of a lock of hair or beard."*

Tess stopped reading again and said as she realized, "Abe wasn't going to hurt me with those scissors. He was after my hair. He wasn't satisfied with what he got out of my brush." Then continued to read, *"The subject is often unaware of their 'admirer' and continues to feed the patient's need to be closer and closer, as the patient tries to insinuate themselves into the subject's life."*

Tess put the letter onto her lap and looked over at Noah. "Well, that's pretty much how it went, I think. I never saw Abe, but he did show up occasionally. And he knew about you and I," she finished before picking up the letter to read more. *"This devotion to the subject does not always indicate sexual motivation but this aspect seems to be one of the most common. There has been some of these intense occurrences between the same sex. Females, although less common, can develop this same sort of disturbed behavior. The mental state of these patients seems to cross gender lines and are found to be as extreme in either sex."*

Tess said, thinking about what she had read, "I guess I should feel better that Abe didn't seem to fixate on me as a sexual object, but he did seem jealous of you and angry at Robert."

She continued, "He ends with his findings, *I haven't found a cure for this disease or brain malfunction. It does not seem to have a connection to any form of tumor or aneurism, but usually escalates to the point where the patient has no way of escape. These things usually end tragically in a murder/suicide when the patient cannot acquire his or her desire."*

Tess put down the letter. "Not a very happy ending is that? He certainly leaves no room for hope that Abe will simply melt away into the night."

"What's all that other stuff?" Noah asked.

"They're articles from scientific journals, findings and studies of mental illness that have criminal outcomes. I'll go over them tomorrow when I can take notes," she said folding the letter back together.

"We haven't seen hide or hair of Abe. Everyone in town knows I'm looking for him and so does every lawman for several towns around. I don't think Abe's dumb enough to try to come back here to get you. Maybe it's a good thing you'll be leaving to get your degree."

She knew Noah was trying to make her feel better about leaving him and Abe behind.

"Unless he steamed one of my letters to the university open before sending it on the stage," she said, putting all her worries out in front of them.

"I was hoping you hadn't thought about that. Abe might have easily steamed open all your mail to get closer to you, know what was going on even before you did." Noah said, "Hell, I'm trying to make you feel safer now you've finally begun to smile again. Then I go and agree Abe may be ahead of us." He studied her face before asking, "Do you want me to stay in the house? I won't need to sleep with you unless you want me to."

She looked at him remembering their agreement for the two of them to be circumspect with their relationship and maintain separate homes. Noah always slept in his own bed, even after Tess visited him. She didn't want them to set up housekeeping where a patient seeking help might come upon them. Each morning, Tess poured him coffee outside on the porch on his way to the office. She fixed him a meal each night, which he helped cleaned-up after before he went home, alone.

"No, you're close enough and we have, Buddy. I don't think he thinks of Abe as a friend any longer, not after he locked him up in Robert's room." She scratched the dog's ears as he lay on her feet.

"I changed all the locks in case Abe had a key, too. I wouldn't put it past Robert to have passed them out like candy. I found out that Dorothy and the Reverend had keys so who knows who else did. I don't know what he was thinking," Noah said derisively shaking his head.

"He was thinking what a nice safe town Forever is, having such a handsome, wonderful and devoted sheriff."

"I hope not, I don't salute another flag," he said letting the lighter mood end the discussion they both hated to face. The one that will happen when she obtained her acceptance to finish university.

Still unsettled by the letter she received, he said, "I wouldn't put too much into what this doctor says, Doc. I mean, he's in a city where people don't care about and protect one another. I'm watching out for you and so is Andrew and a couple of others. They don't know the whole story, but they know to tell me if Abe shows up. If they even think he may be back around. I'm not going to let him just stroll back into town."

Yet that's pretty much how it happened.

CHAPTER EIGHTEEN

After the first few days of being kept locked away in her home, Tess thought it safe enough to visit Meredith. She met with Meredith after church in the parsonage. Tess watched the excitement run through her friend as Meredith described her last meeting with Andrew. How Meredith hoped things would progress. It seemed Andrew was more than willing to be considered Meredith's beau. The stage didn't come into town daily and there was talk of getting a telegraph office soon, which would cut down on the amount of mail the stage carried. Meredith worried Andrew would leave if there were even less stages into town.

Tess tried to calm her friend. "If Andrew has feelings for you, as I suspect he does, he'll find a way for you to be together. I'm sure of it."

"I hope you're right. We haven't been seeing one another that long but I know he's the one. And he's been right here under my nose the whole time." Meredith fidgeted with her yarn and needles which was unlike her usually calm demeanor.

"Well, you're both rather shy. That's probably why you feel so right together."

"I think he's keeping something from me. Do you think he's trying to tell me he's leaving?"

Tess knew Andrew was one of the people Noah had taken into his confidence. How to shelter Meredith from harsh reality and keeping Abe's actions a secret? "I don't think Andrew would do anything so ungentlemanly. He probably has more on his mind with the extra duties at his job. He'll tell you everything, I'm sure, when he feels able."

"I'm simply so unsure of him, right now. You're the one with experience knowing men. I'll have to take your word on things." Meredith smiled and continued knitting as Tess did the same.

Wishing she could confide in Meredith Tess knew it would only frighten her friend that someone so dangerous had been living there among them. It was better, Tess thought, if the true reason behind Abe's leaving wasn't made public.

Tess stopped by the general store for a few needed items. As she boxed up the order, Dorothy commented on the increased amount of food Tess was purchasing.

Without a blink of an eye, Tess explained, "This time of year I make soups and such and can them. I'm so much busier in the colder weather when everyone gets coughs or influenza. I don't get time to make a meal. That reminds me, I need a box of new lids, please."

Dorothy smiled at being able to increase her sale and added it all up accepting the money from Tess.

Other than Tess sending Noah to the store some of the time, not much changed in the town. This way, Noah was still buying groceries and Tess was back to buying her usual amount. One gossipmonger sidestepped.

Noah asked one night after dinner, "When are you going to have to box up all this stuff?" He glanced around the room. "Does Robert want the furniture shipped, too?"

"No, I decided to buy it. Millicent saw the furniture when she was here and thought she wanted something more current. Something imported, I think. I really believe Robert's need to sell the equipment or the entire place was due to money issues. He's buying into a practice in St. Louis, but he's lowest in seniority. He'll need to work his way up to become one of the actual partners. He's had little to no surgical experience and that's where the money is in those large cities."

She could see Noah thinking about what she had told him. He asked as if the answer didn't have any consequences, "Just how well off did that late husband of yours leave you?"

Knowing Noah never asked irrelevant questions, Tess answered, "I'm not an heiress or anything but I have enough to do what I need to do."

"And what is it you think you need to do? That is, besides get that little piece of paper?" he asked, probing into places he never dared enter before.

She wasn't sure if this was the right time for this conversation but he would need to know eventually. She had hoped that time would be after she earned her degree.

"Carter, I'm a surgeon. In a town like Forever there isn't room for more than one doctor so I'm prepared to take care of all the town's health needs. My talent, my training is in surgery. I plan to open a clinic that would be able to handle surgeries as well as everyday injuries and illness. To have a full operating theatre to save the lives of people in this area who don't have the means to travel all the way to Austin or further to find proper medical help."

Watching his reaction to her words, she felt it safe to continue. "Right now, people are dying from illnesses others are being saved from in larger cities. That's not right in my mind. I can furnish the needed expertise and hire assistants and nurses for after care."

"Tell me again how much money you have?" he asked now appearing more curious.

"Doctor McLeish and I were very busy training in the hospital surgery, but we made most of our money from speaking engagements, books and medical periodicals. We then invested our money so we could serve more people. A McLeish is frugal if nothing else." She smiled at the quote she must have heard from her husband a dozen times a week.

She needed to make sure Noah understood. "It was our passion to make these surgeries, that have the potential to prevent so many deaths, available to everyone who needs them. We donated our time and skill to people who would otherwise have been turned away."

"I just don't want you to think I can't provide for you, Doc." He appeared worried that finances might come between them. "I don't think I have as much as you do but you won't want for anything."

"It never crossed my mind you couldn't, Carter. Don't think about my money, think about what it will mean for the people here to have access to a clinic, almost a full hospital with beds and all the newest medical equipment and care." She wanted him to understand her need to do this, and yet, she didn't want him to feel she didn't need him because she had wealth of her own.

"That's the way I'll see things then. I just can't wait for you to get done with this school business. You'll come back so we can be married and we won't have to sleep in separate houses." He rubbed his thumb in small circles on the hand he reached over to hold.

Caressing him with her eyes, she wanted to agree. "Time will pass quickly, I hope. I'll do whatever extra work that is needed to finish as soon as I can." Her voice softened as his touch made her think of things beside school.

"So, if we hurry up with the dishes will you be over this evening?" he asked hopefully.

Tess drew the corners of her mouth down. "I'm indisposed for the next few days."

Noah drew his brows down as he frowned at this news. "We can maybe do something…."

"No, we will not. I'm afraid you're on your own this evening." She couldn't stop the laugh that erupted at the expression of bewildered loss that crossed his face.

"I was just going to suggest we sleep together, Doc, nothing more, I promise."

"I'm sleeping here and you're sleeping way over there," she said pointing to his house out the window. "Now help me clear up and I'm sending you home."

Turning out the lamp in the kitchen, he kissed her before leaving through the back door which Tess locked after he was on the porch. He tipped his hat as if giving her one more chance to change her mind and go home with him but she merely waved.

A knocking on the front door a half hour later had Tess going to see who was there this late. Looking out the small window to the side of the door, she saw the top of a man's ten-gallon hat as he bent over a baby wrapped in a blanket.

Tess immediately wrenched open the door and was suddenly pushed backwards against the stairs, their wooden treads cutting into her back as she landed. What she thought was a baby dropped harmlessly to the floor - just a bag of rags.

It took her a moment to clear her head. "Abe, you better leave right now. I'm not going anywhere with you and you need to know your plans are not going to become real. I want you to stop and think rationally about what you're doing," she said loudly and slowly, hoping Noah hadn't gone straight to bed.

"I know I did things wrong before. I can see that now. I scared you, I'm sorry. I didn't mean to. I'm better now, I won't hurt you again," Abe said, his eyes darting everywhere while not settling on any one thing. He was dressed as a cowhand and wore a side-arm in a holster.

Searching around, too, Tess tried to figure out why Buddy wasn't there making a nuisance of himself. At least getting under her feet if the dog still thought Abe was a friend as Tess had told him several weeks ago.

Slamming the front door, Abe got her full attention. "I need you to pack so we can leave, Forever. I've found us a farmhouse and we can make a nice little family there. I'll be good to you, Sweetheart. Do you need any help packing?" he asked almost as if he were the courteous fiancé, he thought himself to be.

"No, I can manage. May I pack some of my medical equipment? They could come in handy if one of us gets hurt or I can make money if someone else needs help," she fabricated, trying to take more time packing, possibly finding a way to escape or for Noah to notice her lamps on later than usual.

"No, wait...I'm not sure," he said, his agitation increasing now that his plan was threatened.

"I'll pack my things upstairs then, until you decide." She tried to think if she could warn Noah through Robert's window. Or, possibly, climb out her own and let herself down to drop the rest of the way. Two stories aren't that far to fall, she thought, trying to make plans to escape.

"I'll come with you. Help get your trunk and cases out of the box room." Abe took her arm to help her up the stairs, walking to her side. Tess made different plans now she knew she wasn't going to be left alone.

"Will we need any furnishings like linen or kitchen items? There's a wooden crate on the back porch we can pack." Tess tried to discourage his following her upstairs and impeding her escape.

"No, we can get those things on the way. I don't want to take that much time here. The sheriff might wake up." Tess got a chill down her spine.

"Did you do something to Noa... the sheriff, then? Did you hit him again?" she asked now worrying about Noah, another hard blow could be dangerous for him.

"No, he's snoring louder than a freight train. I can't believe you can sleep through it." Taking her to the end of the hall, he opened the box room and pulled a wooden trunk out of it.

"That one will be fine, I'll take that one," Tess said pointing to one of the largest ones. Abe didn't see anything wrong with her choice and dragged it to the bedroom so she could pack.

Tess began to pack her underskirts, neatly folded the dresses she brought with her and the ones Millicent gave her. Her cape and boots were next. They weren't taking up much of the trunk space so she folded and packed the bed cover and a couple of her pillows, and covered them with the last dress and the items from her two drawers. It wasn't full but it was fairly heavy.

She slammed the lid closed. "That's it for up here. Have you decided if I can take any of the medical supplies?"

"Not this time. Maybe we can come back and get them. I want to leave as soon as I carry this out." He ordered Tess, "Go down the steps and out the front door to the wagon waiting there. I'll follow with the trunk."

Tess tried to judge her ability to outrun him and damned her long skirts. Even holding those up, they would slow her down. Abe must be fast since he seemed to be able to disappear so quickly, before. Peering around for the best place to run to, she decided it was probably to Noah when Abe yelled out behind her.

"Where the hell are the horses and wagon?" He dropped the trunk and searched the darkness.

"Right where I left them," Carter said, pulling Tess away from Abe's reach. He told her quietly, "Stay behind me. He could pull that gun and start shooting anytime."

Tess wished there was something she could think of to disarm the situation. Nothing came to mind that didn't put someone in more danger. She looked down the main street towards the saloon, the only place where anyone would still be awake. It was dark and silent.

Backing away, she figured if Noah didn't need to

protect her, he might be able to get the gun from Abe without any shots being fired. Abe didn't seem to realize how much farther behind the sheriff Tess was, but she thought Noah did.

Noah yelled, "Run, Doc!" He heard her footsteps receding from him.

Abe startled as he looked around. "Doctor Waverly? You here?" Then seemed to realize Carter had called out to Tess. Abe now searched the darkness to find her. He appeared worried and frightened when he couldn't discover her.

"You ruin everything, Sheriff. Why didn't you just stay away from her. Then she and I could live our lives together, like Doctor Waverly wanted us to," he whined and pleaded at the same time.

Noah didn't want to have to shoot the man because he would shoot to kill. Wounded Abe was more dangerous. He couldn't give a wounded man the chance to shoot him in retaliation no matter how unstable the man was.

"Let's just talk this over, Abe. We used to be friends and we can be again. It's not like you've done anything wrong here, yet."

The young man who was sweating now he realized his plans had gone awry once again.

Squinting into the darkness, Abe still seemed unable to see Tess. He started shaking and whined yet again.

"All I want is for Mrs. McLeish and me to be together. We're supposed to be together. Doctor Waverly told me so."

That remark made Noah ask, "Doctor Waverly told you to come and take her? Take Mrs. McLeish?"

"He said he had fallen in love with that Major Phillip's daughter. Said he felt bad about bringing Mrs. McLeish all this way then not marrying her. I said I would, you know marry her. Doctor Waverly said he'd be ever so grateful to any man who'd take her off his hands and leave him to marry the other one," Abe explained in the most coherent sentences yet that night, thought Carter.

"Well, Doctor Waverly did marry Major Phillip's daughter and they live happily in St. Louis. I'm going to marry Te, Mrs. McLeish and will stay here, happily. So, everyone is married and everyone is happy. Now will you give me your gun and we can all go back to our beds?" Noah asked in quiet tones.

Abe stood, slightly swaying. "But then I don't have anyone. No one that cares about me. Doctor Waverly left me and Mrs. McLeish likes you and not me, anymore. I don't want to live if I don't have someone." Abe sniveled sounding like a spoiled child.

Before Noah could decide what to do next, Abe suddenly pulled the gun from its holster. There was a loud shot and a flash of light in the night.

"Damn," Noah said as he strode forward kicking the side arm out of the fallen man's hand.

Tess came running over from the building across the street where she had been hiding. "Oh, you had to shoot him? Can I help him?"

"I just wounded him. He was going to shoot himself and it was the only way to stop him. I think you can help him, but don't make him fall in love with you all over again. Anyone being nice to him and he thinks he's infatuated or something." Noah was trying to figure out how to lift the young man and do the least amount of damage.

"I heard a gunshot, that you, Sheriff? Need any help?" Andrew asked coming out of the darkness carrying a long rifle. His trousers were pulled on with the suspenders over bare shoulders and boots shoved on in haste.

"Grab his legs and we'll take him to the Doc's room." Noah grasped Abe under his arms lifting him from the ground.

Tess followed the three men and as she began to pull open drawers and doors said, "Somehow I knew I would be needing my medical supplies this evening."

She leaned over her unconscious patient, cutting the sleeve off his shirt exposing the wound to his shoulder. "Carter, I won't need an assistant, but make sure his feet are tied. I'm so tired of having him try to kidnap me I'm finding it difficult to remember my Hippocratic Oath."

Looking at Noah, Andrew smiled saying, "Good to know you do have your limits, Doctor. I was beginning to think you were a saint. I don't know how you held back from killing him, Sheriff. He seems to have given you ample reasons."

"I know but a doctor sent us information explaining this was a mental illness, something Abe has no control over so I have to treat him as such. Maybe he'll get better where I'll take him as soon as Te, the Doc gets him fixed up."

Andrew nodded and left saying, "I'll see ya in the mornin' then."

Tess looked up from her suturing, smiling at Noah. "I'm proud you took the information we received to heart. Found it within yourself to try to help Abe."

"He not awake, yet?" Noah deflected attention from himself as Tess finished taping the bandage in place.

"It's like he doesn't want to wake up. In shock, I suppose. Maybe catatonic. I'm not that experienced with illnesses of the mind." She watched Noah tie Abe's hands to the line wrapped around his ankles.

"We'll stay here till daybreak when Andrew is bringing me a wagon. I'm going to take him to Palo Duro which is the closest facility that takes the criminally insane."

"I hope he gets help. It kind of breaks my heart knowing he's lost in a make-believe world. Can't find his way out." She showed too much concern for a man who tried to abduct her – twice. "I can't seem to retain my anger at him. After all, he was one of the first people I met in Forever."

"He could have done a lot worse if you weren't able to keep your head and talk with him. You kept him from doing something horrible. We have to remember he also has a great capacity to do harm." Noah hugged her to his chest, saying a prayer of thanks that Buddy's scratching and whining woke him up in time.

The couple stepped apart and Tess said, "Let me get some food packed for the trip. There's not going to be many places for you and a prisoner to stop along the way."

"No, I don't suppose there will be," was Carter's quiet reply.

CHAPTER NINETEEN

Again, the town ate up news of the events that happened in the middle of the night. No one knew exactly what occurred because those who were the closest to the action weren't talking. Tess was again at the general store and had to endure Dorothy's inquisition.

"Is the sheriff back, yet?" That nosy woman asked trying to get information for her daily hangers-on.

"Is he gone? I don't really see him much. Mostly coming home from work, but I've been busy with patients lately," Tess admitted honestly. She didn't say most of those patients were seeking information about that gun shot in the middle of the night and the missing sheriff.

"I thought you were closer than that. I mean he gave you that scruffy mutt, didn't he?" Dorothy continued as she placed items in a box for another customer who was avidly listening to the conversation.

"Sheriff Carter probably got tired of hearing me scream every time I saw a mouse. Buddy is a great guard dog and even chases the rodents out of my garden area. I don't know what I would do without him even if he is a bit scruffy looking," Tess answered without answering.

"I thought…."

Before Dorothy could continue along that vein, Tess spoke up, "Isn't it exciting about Meredith Jenkins and Andrew becoming engaged? Now who would have seen that coming?"

Dorothy took the gambit as Tess hoped, silently apologizing to her friend for using her upcoming wedding as a distraction from Carter and herself.

After walking the gauntlet of grocery shoppers, Tess continued home and put everything away. Looking across at the empty house behind the jail, she hoped the many days away didn't mean Noah had trouble getting Abe committed to a facility. Abe could appear quite sane at times and Noah had no proof other than his own word.

Tess brought in the clean, dry sheets from the line and began folding them bending over the examination table as she did so. Two strong arms came around her from the back and a hoarse whisper in her ear said, "I sure did miss you, Doc." Noah kissed her neck and the side of her face.

Tess leaned back into his muscular body, craning her neck to give him even more access whispering in return, "I missed you, too. I'm glad you're back. I was beginning to get worried."

Her hands covered his forearms as he placed one hand on each breast pressing gently, letting her feel his arousal against her backside.

"I missed that, too," Tess said pushing into him and grinding against him, knowing he would enjoy her eager welcome.

"I locked the door. Can I, can we maybe...?" he pleaded, kissing and sucking at her neck.

"I'd like that, too," she whispered rejoicing in his attentions, reaching back, and pressing his erection against her hand.

Tess smiled as she heard Noah removing his holster one handed and letting it drop, then work at getting his belt buckle undone. He became quiet and leaned his head against hers.

"What's wrong?"

"I didn't plan on... I don't have any protection," he told her dejectedly.

"There's some in the top drawer behind you. I ordered a gross."

With humor in his voice and fumbling behind her he replied, "That's my girl, although a gross is quite a formidable number to be faced with."

Then pulling up her skirts from behind, he entered her without hesitation. Tess arched her back, jubilant in having him within her once more. It didn't take long for them to reach their euphoric conclusion. Tess fell forward over the table while Noah tried to hold some of his own weight off her.

"I really wanted that. I missed you so much I had tonight all planned out. Then I saw you here, alone, and all my good intentions went right out the window." He kissed her along her jaw line.

Standing, he turned Tess into his arms and kissed her lips taking his fill of her now the immediacy of desire was taken care of. "I meant to just tell you what happened. Needed to let you know Abe is behind bars and won't be getting out anytime soon."

"So, there won't be a trial?" Tess stood within his arms allowing her gaze to travel over his face that was so dear to her.

"No, but I was worried there for a minute. By the time we got to Palo Duro he was almost acting normal, as if we were old friends, telling me he forgave me for shooting him. Like it was all a misunderstanding or something. I had to talk like hell before they would lock him up." Noah kissed the tip of her nose and finished, "But being locked up kind of got him riled and the crazy talk began and it was all over for him. I left him with the professionals and warned them not to turn their backs on him."

"It's sad in so many ways, but I'm glad you're home and I won't need to keep locking up every time I step outside."

They walked into the parlor now they were both presentable again.

"I learned something on this trip, Doc." Tess smiled at his calling her Doc after everything they had been doing. "I'm going with you when you have to go back to Michigan. I won't go through missing you and worrying about you like I have been. Do you think you can put up with me? I know we won't have any time together, but at least I'll be able to see you and watch over you."

"But your job is here and you're a Texan through and through. Michigan, where I'll be living, is green and you can't go more than a mile before running into a lake or pond or river. There's a lot of farms but no cattle, just milk cows." At Noah's grimace, she continued honestly, "I don't want you miserable and I swear I won't look at another man."

"Yeah, but they will be looking at you. I know you'll be in the student quarters, but I would feel better knowing I could see you every once in a while, maybe after church or something," he said kissing her, holding her hand, seemingly needing to keep the connection between them.

"You're letting this past trip get on your nerves. I haven't even been accepted back and it's already into August. I may not be going anywhere."

"I want you to have your dreams Tess, but I can't say I'm sad you don't have a date to leave me yet," he said trying to cover a yawn.

"Go and rest and maybe get cleaned-up. You have a little more than stubble and I don't want any whisker burn tomorrow," she watched the light in his eyes flare with desire again. "Go, now! I'll have supper ready at the usual time."

CHAPTER TWENTY

Tess, anxious to get the answer to her application to the university, often stopped by the stage office to check for mail and talk with Andrew. Of course, she often found Meredith there, as well, simply spending time with her fiancé.

"Oh, Tess I know you're worried about going to university again but I would love to have you stand up with me as my maid of honor. Andrew is going to ask the sheriff to be his best man," she said as if Tess needed that as an incentive.

"If I'm here then I would be honored to do so, but I need to finish a couple of classes before I can continue with my plans to open a clinic," Tess explained, hoping her friend understood the importance of her leaving for university.

"When I set the date to be the same as my parent's anniversary, I didn't think about you not being in Forever in September. I've already told so many people and my aunt has already made plans to come then," Meredith said with regret.

"Don't change your whole wedding on account of me, Meredith. You know my best wishes will be with you even if I can't be." She spoke to the couple since she was very fond of Andrew ever since that night he helped with Abe and evidently hadn't told anyone.

Andrew chuckled. "I'd be willing to move up the wedding date. We could do something special on Meredith's parent's anniversary instead."

"We would have been married the day after you asked me if I let you have your way," she teased her husband-to-be.

"Well, ladies it's time for me to close up this office and open the livery. I wear so many hats lately I have a difficult time taking one off and putting the other on," Andrew said as he began to lock up. "I can walk with you both if you're heading for the rectory."

"That will be fine. I'll head back with Meredith and she can show me how far she's gotten on her wedding dress. I can help her decide on the hat." Tess walked beside her friend who received a kiss right out on the street when Andrew left them to take care of the horses.

"I'm so glad I listened to you, Tess. I could have lost this chance at being happy, of finding a man I know I was meant to be with for the rest of my life. I don't know how to thank you." Meredith confided once they were sitting in the rectory's parlor, the reverend on his daily calls to members of his congregation who couldn't make it to Sunday worship.

"I'll put water on for tea. Then I'll get the pictures of the hats I've been having trouble deciding over." Meredith left as Tess picked up a slim catalog of wedding finery, such as clocked stockings and gossamer veils with pearls sewn around the border. All lovely items, it was no wonder Meredith was having trouble making decisions.

"Tes-s-s," a wavering voice came from the kitchen, a tone Tess had never heard Meredith use before. As Tess stood to see what the matter was, Meredith shuffled into the parlor, her face white and her lips thin with fear. Abe, now with a full beard and mustache which made him appear much older, was right behind her. Holding a kitchen knife pressed to Meredith's neck he held his prisoner by one arm.

"Abe, how nice to see you again. Are you feeling better?" Tess asked edging toward the couple but was stopped at Abe's command.

"Stay right there! No one will get hurt, I promise. I never meant to hurt anyone," he said explaining away all his previous actions.

"I understand, Abe, and I am willing to go with you as soon as you let Meredith go. She's not part of this and should be left out of it." Tess tried to speak reasonably to the unreasonable man.

"I will as soon as we take a trip, all of us together, Mrs. McLeish. You know I can't hurt you, not on purpose. I never meant for you to get hurt." He shook Meredith to make a point. "I don't have the same feelings about your friend. She'll go with us until I can trust you to stay with me. I still have that farm where we can all live. Once we're married, and you are carrying my child, I'll set your friend, Meredith, free," he told them, seemingly having all their lives planned for the next few months.

"Meredith is due to get married. She needs to stay and help the reverend with his work. She can't leave right now, but I can. Are we getting horses from the livery?" Tess tried to divert Abe's plans to take Meredith with them. Thinking it would be easier to rescue one rather than two without someone getting hurt.

"We're all going together. I already have a buggy so we can leave right now." He jerked Meredith's arm as she stared at Tess fearfully.

"Then we'll need to get some things together for the trip. For our stay at the farm," Tess said. She was glad to see the color returning to her friend's cheeks. Tess felt Meredith was beginning to try to out think Abe, too, now and was figuring out ways to get free. Tess was hoping her friend would take any opportunity to escape.

Probably remembering the last time, he got caught after letting Tess pack the trunk, Abe said, "We'll get them later. I want to leave now before anyone sees me."

"Well, we are females and we need female things with us. Do you understand?" Tess said planning on making female's needs more obvious if the young man was too ignorant to know about such things. She didn't need to explain more although he seemed to be unsure what all was required. Tess hoped Meredith would use his uncertainty to her advantage.

Abe's cheeks and ears flushed red as he nodded. He let Meredith go. That young woman slid her feet sideways to further the distance between the knife and herself.

"Go and pack your personal items, Meredith. Make sure you get the things hanging out to dry," Tess told her friend hoping she would run once outside the house.

"No, just what's here and remember, I cut Tess once before and I'll do it again." He explained to the anxious women, "I won't go back to that place, ever. They have some really bad men there, men that are crazy with madness."

He motioned Meredith towards the bedrooms, saying, "I'll take Tess the hard way if you give anyone a warning. Just get those things you need so we can leave."

Tess tried to make Meredith understand she should run no matter what the mad man said. Leave Tess to handle Abe. But her friend was too loyal and wouldn't accept the one chance of escape. Going into her room, Meredith began opening drawers but made no attempt to leave through a window as Tess had prayed, she would.

"How did you get out?" Tess was interested as well as trying to keep Abe's mind off Meredith.

"I simply waited a day or two then left as a visiting doctor after tying the real one up. None of those guards ever looked at us so no one knew me. I just waited for the guards to change shifts then left with a smile wearing the doctor's clothes. It wasn't difficult." He seemed to want to brag about his escape, preened in her interest.

"When I got to a town with a Weber & Weber stagecoach line, I told them I was C. J. Weber, one of the owners and demanded to be taken to Forever. No one even questioned me because no one wanted the boss to know they didn't recognize him from Adam. I got here in record time and all for free." He laughed at his ex-fellow employees for their gullibility.

"That was very inventive and brave of you, Abe. I must say I'm flattered at the lengths you've gone to be near my side. I had no idea your feelings ran so deep." Tess kept his attention as best she could.

Abe looked at her as if unsure she was spinning tales as she had once before or telling him the truth, which he so wanted it to be. In his inability to find the truth, he yelled into the bedroom, "You've taken enough time. We need to be leaving now. Get out back to the buggy."

Meredith came out of her room with a carpetbag in her hand. There didn't appear to be much in it. The two women led the way through the kitchen and porch to the single-horse buggy tied to the back railing. Meredith got up onto the seat when she was ordered while Abe held onto Tess's arm. He ordered Tess to the driver's side pushing her up the step. Raising his foot, Abe evidently planned on following her onto the bench seat, bringing the reins with him.

The sound of a rifle-shot rang out from the distance. Abe dropped unto his back in the dust. Both women jumped with the surprise of his fall.

Unable to repress her instinct to help an injured person no matter who it was, Tess climbed down to give aid. She felt for a pulse but knew it wasn't necessary. The hole in his forehead had definitely been a kill shot.

Tess turned, looking up to see Meredith losing all sense of bravery and crying into her hands. Andrew rushed up huffing, set down a long-gun and held out his arms to his fiancée. Falling into them, Andrew cradled Meredith to his chest. He whispered little hushing sounds in her hair as she cried out the shock of the past half-hour.

Noah came running from around the side of the house, handgun ready, but realized the danger was past as he saw Tess still kneeling by the body. "How the hell did he get out so soon? He nearly beat me back here." He pulled Tess up into his arms for comfort.

Tess recovered first. Knowing shock would soon set in for everyone, she ushered Andrew and Meredith into the house. Taking the now boiling water, she made strong tea with extra sugar. Then made everyone drink it, including herself. There were no spirits in the rectory so they had to make do with what was at hand.

Meredith began to realize it had been Andrew who shot Abe from a distance. "How did you do that? How did you know I needed help?" she asked while sitting next to him on the sofa, the trembling finally lessening.

"I was told a wild story by the stagecoach driver as I exchanged horses. He bragged he had one of the coach-line owners in his coach for the past two days, a C. J. Weber. But I know the only Mr. Weber still alive and he's over seventy. He's not about to be thrown about a coach just to get here. When the Shotgun told me the man was young, I knew something was up. There are no young family members in the company. Neither Weber's ever married."

He squeezed her to his side. "It took me a while to find him. When I did, he was pushing you into that buggy, which I didn't like at all. You didn't have on your hat or gloves and you never leave the house without them," he smiled at the silly little things that went through his mind.

Noah asked, "You didn't recognize him as Abe? I mean, I saw him with a beard so I didn't have a problem knowing him right off, but the rest of you haven't."

"I did once I got him in my sight," Andrew admitted.

"How did you pull off that shot with the ladies so near?" Noah seemed impressed and Tess waited for the answer as well.

"I learned to shoot distances during the war. I was only in for a few months before it ended, but have used that rifle to turkey shoot since then. It was a natural skill, my Sergeant told me back then." Andrew shrugged, not assuming it was any great feat. "I knew when he climbed up, he'd be more than a foot higher than the women and a clear shot for me. I took it. I wasn't about to find out what his intentions were. I knew he wasn't right in the head, but that didn't make him any less dangerous."

Carter shook his head. "No, you did the right thing, Andrew. I hoped the place where I left him could have made something of him, but his madness was too strong, I guess. I'm just glad no one else got hurt this time."

Carter glanced over at Meredith then at her as if making a comparison of the wilting puddle in Andrew's arms and herself. Tess knew she would feel badly over this outcome even though it was inevitable.

"I'll take the Doc home and get a wagon to return Abe. The state can contact any family members to find out where they should send the body. That all right with you, Doc?" Noah asked.

"Yes. Andrew stay with Meredith until her brother gets home, please. Tell him to send for me if she is still too upset to sleep. I can give her something to help with that." Tess stood and left with a quiet Noah.

They walked silently to their end of the main street, the businesses and houses becoming fewer and fewer as they reached their last two buildings. "I'm sorry things turned out the way they did, Tess."

"I know you are, Carter. I mean you spent days getting him to a place where you thought they could help him. He wasn't ready to be helped. I hope he didn't kill the doctor who was trying to relieve his symptoms." Tess felt depressed thinking of all the harm one man could do and still not be a monster.

Once behind closed doors at the doctor's office, Tess turned to Noah and cried her fears and sadness out. Sad for all the fear and unrest Abe caused, sad for her friend who might have this trauma effect her relationship with her fiancé, sad because a sick, confused young man was dead. And sad because her own stalwart man would leave to take the body back once more to its final resting place.

Tess, worn out from the trauma and tears, told Noah he should leave and remove the body from the rectory's back yard. She agreed it would be best to take the body back to the state prison, which had rights over it. No one in town knew of any family so the state should have control. Fewer bad memories for the townspeople, too. Let them remember Abe as the nice young man who ran the ticket office and delivered their mail and packages when the stage came in Forever.

CHAPTER TWENTY-ONE

Buddy knew something bad happened and whined to get up onto the sofa, a thing Tess usually didn't allow. But the furniture was hers now and she wanted the warm comfort that this furry friend could provide. Tess decided to try to sleep although the problems of the day and having Noah absent again would make getting and staying asleep difficult.

She heard a shot ring out and Tess snapped awake. Buddy lying next to her continued to give his little doggie snores and she realized the rifle-shot had been in her dream or rather nightmare. She couldn't remember anything else, just the rifle-shot and her knowledge that she must wake-up, be aware of her surroundings.

Laying back, she listened to the quiet night, the night she would need to get used to again. This time there really wasn't any way Abe could return. Only in her nightmares, only if she gave him access to her mind. She said a prayer for his soul and knew she would never dream of him again. Abe was dead and all the memories will be buried with him.

Noah returned two days later, unbathed, unshaved and much awaited. Tess saw him walk up the path between their homes and ran out. He looked around and gave her a kiss on the lips but apologized about his condition.

"It's a little difficult to get anyone to rent you a room on the road when one of the occupants is dead, I found out. A lot easier the first time I took him in. Then on the way back I didn't want to stop so tried to ride right through. Now you're paying the price because I need a bath, badly." He made a face as if he couldn't stand to be near himself.

"Let me help you heat the water. It won't take that long," Tess offered, glad to have him home in any condition.

"No," he said grinning. "But I'll let you watch me from your back porch. This may be the last night warm enough to take a bath outside. I'll have to return to bathing in front of the stove."

Tess looked at him with narrowed eyes, sensing a scheme. "Did you just start to bathe outside when I moved in?"

"The weather was getting warm and it is easier to dump the water off the end of the porch. Besides, it waters the weeds that way, too." He laughed out loud at her affronted dignity.

"You are a scoundrel! I knew it the day I met you." She was smiling, too, at his admittance he had been trying to get her attention from the beginning. And it worked because there weren't too many things, she enjoyed more than watching him take a bath.

"And you love me," he teased back. They both got quiet, the truth too close, his eyes intense as they gazed into hers.

"And I love watching you take a bath. Don't let me down, Carter, I'm expecting something that will make my socks roll down." She took pleasure in the intense heat of desire as it passed over his face.

"Then hold on to your stockings, Doc. I'm going to have your eyes popping and you drooling to get your hands on me by the time I'm done tonight." He tipped his Stetson and walked backwards, never letting his gaze leave hers all the way to his back porch.

Noah was as good as his word. He lathered up the stubble on his face and made a long ritual of shaving, letting the extra suds drip onto his bare chest and run down to the top of his trousers which were beltless and sitting low on his hips. The top two buttons open and undone, a dark mass of hair visible even as far away as Tess's porch.

After filling the tub with water off his stove, he let his trousers drop before turning full frontal towards Tess. Her mouth went dry with want. But she remained in her chair, anxious to see what more he had planned for her, for them, since she knew he enjoyed teasing her with his nakedness. Even though she had seen more naked men than any one woman could boast about, this one man meant everything to her.

Climbing into the tub gave her an inadvertent view of his muscled backside, the thrusting muscles she loved to smooth her hands over when they made love. She smiled at his antics, lifting his leg out of the bath water in ways he had never done before to soap and rinse it.

The sun lowered out of sight but they could see one another. The only light was the lamp in her kitchen window behind her and his lamp on the porch behind his tub. Tess began to unbutton the little pearl buttons one by one and open the camisole's ribbon at the same time.

Noah stopped his bathing and began to watch with intensity. Feeling his gaze hot on her, she raised a leg in the air as he had allowing her skirts to slip to her hip.

She rolled the stocking down one then the other leg leaving the naked skin exposed as she shimmied out of the petticoats she had untied from around her waist.

Just then she was swept up against a chest still dripping with water, droplets falling from his hair unto her as she squealed and wriggled in vain against Noah's cold, wet body.

"Noah you're naked, put me down," she ordered uselessly as he carried her back across the yard and into his house where a lone lamp lit the living area. Carrying her into the bedroom, he dropped her to bounce on the mattress held up by ropes.

"Now you're paying for interrupting my bath and making me run buck-naked across the yard after you," he growled threateningly.

"I did not make you do any such thing. I was only paying you back for what you were doing to me," she said laughing as he jumped on the bed beside her, his arousal nudged up against her dress buffeting it from her skin.

"I missed you so very much again that it worries me about letting you go north without me. I don't want to interfere with what you want to do, but will you think about letting me come, too? I have some savings and can rent out my farm as well as the grazing lands I have attached to it," he told her holding her close and kissing her. He growled, "I'm tired of waiting for your body."

Tess seemed unable to get enough of him. Unable to stop running her hands over his body. It wasn't long before Noah removed what clothes Tess had left on and they explored each other like new lovers. The evening ended as Noah reached his pinnacle taking Tess with him - both floating slowly back to earth.

The next morning Noah walked over to the doctor's office, a gleam lit his eyes as he glanced at the stockings and petticoats Tess forgot to pick-up on her way to bed last night.

He held his empty cup towards her saying, "You'll have to tell me the secret of why your coffee tastes so much better than the sludge I brew up."

"Always start with a clean pot and strainer and add just a sprinkle of cinnamon in with the coffee grounds." She refilled his cup after he downed the first in three or four swallows as usual.

"You'll have to show me. Maybe at dinner tonight? I can bring back a chicken to roast or ham," he offered, letting his eyes travel up and down her body until her cheeks were warm from desire.

"Chicken, I think, if you please. It can roast while I take care of business." She waited till he walked away before turning and snatching up her under things to take them inside.

Carter returned in less than an hour with the chicken and package Andrew had given him to pass on to Tess knowing she was anxious for something from a university.

"Doc, you might want to open this now," he called out as he came through the front door. Anxiety making him brisk, thinking this box may control his life for the next few years.

"What are you hollering about, Carter?" Tess asked as she came into the room drying her hands. "I'm washing the floors."

He held out the slender parcel about nine by twelve inches, wrapped in brown paper and addressed to Mrs.

McLeish. Tess's hands shook a little as she accepted the package and gently tore open one end sliding the box out. She opened the lid to find an envelope addressed to her nestled-on top of white tissue paper. Removing the envelope, she took a deep breath, seemingly preparing herself for the worse. Opening the letter, she began to scan the single sheet of paper.

Tess was silent so long Carter thought for sure she'd been denied entrance to the university and he wasn't sure he could console her at the same time as his inner-self was yelling for joy.

"Is it, good news?" he asked softly, not wanting to make her cry when she told him she hadn't made it.

"Yes, yes it's very good news. Unbelievably good news," she said tears welling in her eyes and her lips trembling.

Carter stepped forward and touched her arm, trying to pass some of his strength on to her. "If it's such good news, why are you about to burst into tears?" he asked a little harshly.

"Oh, I'm sorry, Carter. Come and sit with me and I'll read you the letter from the dean."

They walked to the sofa and sat next to one another. "It's a different gentleman than was there when I was a student although he writes that he knew both my father and Doctor McLeish. He compliments me on my technique for suturing. Says he has encouraged others to follow my method as published in the National Medical Journal." She let the letter lay in her lap, saying, "I didn't think anyone paid any attention. I never heard back from anyone."

She continued, "He goes on to say he personally watched some of the surgeries Doctor McLeish and I performed. He was impressed with our ability to work so well together as if, and I quote, *'there is one surgeon with four arms'*." She smiled then explained, "Doctor McLeish often described us as such. But we had worked so long together, so many surgeries that we read each other's minds. We never needed to speak during a surgery."

Noah felt himself get angry. No, not angry…jealous of her late husband. Someone she'd been so close with they didn't need language to communicate. But he reminded himself, it was him, his body that made her practically sing with joy. He could read her without her telling him what she liked or what she desired. Once he accepted that fact, Noah could accept the information in the letter. He could be happy for Tess, for what she was going to be able to accomplish once she received her degree.

"He writes that of all his staff, he couldn't find one of them he thought would be able to add to my knowledge and my expertise. If I wanted to return to the university, I could do so as a professor. If not to teach full time, then at least as a regular lecturer or perform surgeries in theatre." She bounced up and down excitedly. "Do you know what this means? Do you know what an honor he just bestowed on me?"

As Tess tore away the tissue paper, she turned the box toward Noah saying proudly, "He declared my lessons complete. He sent me my medical degree and even framed it. I can't believe he did such a generous thing. But if he believes everything, he has written then what else could he do? He even apologized for not realizing I hadn't graduated. He hopes I don't hold any ill will towards him or the university, again asking if I would find time to visit as a guest lecturer."

Tears flowed down Tess's cheeks as she asked, "You know what this means, Noah?"

"I hope it means you don't have to leave me. That you can hang up that framed piece of paper and stay here with me in Forever," he said smiling as he saw the smile widen on her face.

"That and a whole lot more. I'll be able to begin the clinic as soon as I can get the plans drawn up in Austin. I can begin ordering the more complicated equipment and reviewing the journals to find out what has been invented or tested since I've been away from the medical field," she told him excitedly.

"And we can get married, not wait the two years, right?" he asked almost feeling the negative that would be coming from Tess.

"Now we don't need to feel rushed into anything, Noah. I will be busy and won't be able to spend as much time with you as I should as a newlywed. Please, let's wait until we have time for each other" She placed her hand on his arm next to her.

Noah looked down at her hand. "Yeah, I understand. You'll be busy now. I better get back to work, doctor." He smiled and kissed her forehead as he stood and left through the front door.

CHAPTER TWENTY-TWO

Tess had dinner ready and waiting but Noah never came down the path between the houses. Finally, she carved some of the breast meat and put it on a plate for him and put everything else away. They would talk when he came home for dinner.

If Noah came home, he didn't bother to wake Tess.

In the morning, his house remained dark and quiet, no out stretched arm asking for a morning cup of coffee.

Tess sent letters to architects she found advertised in magazines and newspapers to see if any of them would like to bid on building the clinic. She was excited to begin her plans for her future and wanted to discuss things with Noah, but he still wasn't coming home at night.

It had been three days since Tess had received the package that had changed her entire life yet Noah didn't seem to want to share in her happiness.

Finally, just before dark, Tess caught the movement outside the parlor window. She ran to the back porch and called out, "Hey, stranger, do you want a home cooked meal tonight?"

Noah stopped with one foot on his back step then turned with a smile. "I've already eaten, thanks. Just came back to clean up before leaving. Have a nice evening, doctor." Then entered the house, leaving the lamps unlit.

The smiled died on Tess's lips. She turned, hurt that Noah hadn't asked about her plans or how things were going. She returned inside followed by Buddy, who was whining and trying to get her attention. "Not now, Buddy. Go lay down." This was followed by a whine and the small dog going over and laying on his bed, his large black eyes watching her through the doorway.

Tess sat in the dark as well, waiting for Noah to leave, which he never did. So, he lied to me, she thought. Simply so he didn't need to spend time with me? So, he wouldn't need to face me over the table and make small talk he didn't want to make anymore?

She almost decided to go over to his house and seduce him. She knew he wasn't immune to her, not in that way at least. Tonight, she could make him go up in flames, but then what about tomorrow? Could she stand having the cold man Noah had become walk out and head back to work as usual?

Listen to him tell her to have a nice day as she lay in his bed while he dressed to leave? What happened to their easy camaraderie? Their need to sit and talk with each other about the nothing much happening in their day? Tess had many more questions than she had answers.

Meredith knocked on Tess's front door and Tess put on a wide, bright smile and a welcoming hug. She wouldn't think about the first feelings of disappointment when she saw it wasn't Noah at the door.

"I was worried since I haven't seen you for a few days. I thought I better come to the mountain," teased Meredith.

They sat in the sunny parlor, each on one end of the sofa facing one another.

"I'm sorry. It seems just as I think I've gotten everything planned, I get new literature on someone's invention or equipment they are certain I will need in my clinic. I think someone sold my name to these people because they didn't know of me a few weeks ago," Tess complained and vented at the same time.

"Well anytime someone is spending money, there are those who want part of it whether they have anything to offer or not," Meredith said being a supportive friend.

"I know. Some man tried to sell me what is basically a mesmerize machine. It was debunked a hundred years ago as being useless in the medical field. A phonograph would be of more help," Tess said. "Is this about the wedding? I'm sorry I became so wrapped up in the clinic. I've got to be the worse Matron of Honor ever."

"I know you've been busy so I understand, but we are having a walk-through this Friday afternoon. You know, so we will know where to stand and things like that. Although I've been the witness to so many of these things, I can do one with my eyes closed." Meredith laughed at her shared joke.

"Is it this weekend, already? I'm so sorry, Meredith. I became caught up in my own silly plans and time simply flew by. What can I do to help? I feel so badly about not being there for you," Tess said honestly, wishing to take back time and do a better job with her commitment to Meredith and Andrew.

"It's fine. And your plans aren't silly. The clinic is very important to the town. I had plenty of time and Andrew has actually been a big help. He has excellent taste. I think the cake and flowers will be extremely pretty in the rectory after the service. My brother is all nerves about this wedding and I keep telling him it isn't any different than any other - or any more important."

Tess realized what a good friend Meredith was and how gracious during a time she had every right to expect Tess's attention. Tess had allowed her work to take precedence over everything, including her personal relationships. And not only the one between Meredith and her.

Tess admitted, "Still, I'm sorry I didn't stay focused on you. You deserve a better friend."

"I wouldn't even be getting married if it weren't for you urging me to go after what I wanted." Meredith blushed at what she thought as her un-lady-like pursuit of Andrew.

"Women should go after what we want because men never know what we want if we don't tell them," Tess declared boldly.

"I have to agree with you on that. Andrew has since told me he has admired me for years but thought I was too good for him. I'm glad I was brave enough to keep after him." Meredith sat straighter after this revelation.

"What time on Friday and what am I supposed to do on Saturday. I am clearing the week-end for you right now," Tess told her friend and did so mentally, pushing all else out of her mind.

The two of them made arrangements to meet on Friday and again early Saturday. Tess would help Meredith dress and do all the little things brides do before saying goodbye to their single life.

After Meredith left, Tess was alone to think about how fast the last couple of weeks had slipped away, how easy it was to get lost in her project. Forget there were other people in the world she wished to spend time with, wished to kiss, and caress.

Did she have enough courage to go next door after Noah came home carrying the little packets of protection in her hand? Would that be too brazen of an invitation? Would he respond to her or would he politely decline her offer? Tess's face burned with humiliation merely thinking about being turned down or seeing his discomfort while telling her he was too busy right now.

Tess went upstairs to make sure the dresses she needed to wear this weekend were in perfect condition and the matching hat was clean and the feather un-damaged. Picking up her dress shoes, she felt a wave of melancholy wash over her.

Sitting on the bed, tears rolled down her face realizing she forgot about having to meet Noah at the rehearsal and then the wedding this weekend. How was she to face him and not let everyone know her heart was breaking with his loss?

CHAPTER TWENTY-THREE

Meeting Noah again wasn't as bad as Tess feared. She arrived early to help Meredith dress and sooth her nerves, reminding her friend this was simply a walk-through of the service. That Meredith shouldn't worry about making a mistake. Besides, that was why Tess was there, to ensure there were no errors and the wedding progressed as it should.

When the two ladies went over to the church, Tess found the men were already there. It made it easy to say hello to all of them then stay beside Meredith as support. Who was supporting whom wasn't as easy to tell.

It was decided during the last couple of weeks, since Meredith's brother was officiating and needed to be at the altar, Noah was chosen to walk the bride down the aisle as well as be Best Man. The only problem in Tess's mind was Noah would escort Tess back to the front of the church after the ceremony to the receiving line. After that, Tess would be able to escape quickly to greet everyone as they came to the rectory for a short reception.

The Reverend explained every one's roles during the service and the times they would be needed to move or speak.

Tess thought back to the only wedding she had been involved in, which was when she married Doctor McLeish. How different Meredith's wedding to Andrew would be.

With Tess's elderly husband, she had felt like a child standing next to him. Her father had recently died leaving her reeling with loss and loneliness. She and her father had spent most of their time together after years of him ignoring her. Medicine had brought them together, was her father's passion. One he threw himself into after his wife died trying to bring another child into the world.

Doctor McLeish knew Tess, approved of her dedication to medicine and her determination to make a difference in the world through her skill. He often complimented her in front of her father making her grateful for his acknowledgements. When she said, 'I do' she was vowing to do more than marry the man. She was vowing to work toward his same goals and principals.

She brought herself back to the present to meet Noah's gaze realizing he must have watched the emotions flit across her face. Then his attention returned to the Reverend.

Tess had trouble not thinking of the past though. Remembering when she first felt the stirrings of desire. When Noah admitted he desired her too, that he found her beautiful and lovable, that he got hard merely seeing her.

Noting where Noah stood, she stared at the front of his suit pants as if she would be able to see if he still desired her. As her gaze rose, she saw Noah watching her, an inscrutable expression on his face. Feeling herself blushing scarlet, Tess quickly turned back to the bride and groom who were going through their vows. She urged the heat in her face to fade, but no amount of innocent thoughts could wash away the desire that surged through her when she looked at Noah's crotch.

Tess stayed for the meal following the rehearsal that evening. She politely answered the questions put to her by the others about how her clinic was progressing. Everyone asked except Noah, who showed polite interest, but didn't speak with her directly. Tess hoped no one else noticed. She wouldn't be able to explain because she wasn't sure what had happened herself. Noah simply lost interest.

It was expected by the others Noah would walk Tess home since they lived right next door to one another. Noah smiled politely and assured the others it was his pleasure. He walked Tess down the street, but left her at her front door saying he had other things to finish up since he had taken time off during his work day.

Tess thanked him and opened her door, keeping Buddy from jumping out as he must have smelled Noah just off the porch.

"No Buddy, he can't stay. It's just you and me again. Come on and I'll let you out back." Which she did - trying not to look over at the still dark house next door and trying not to cry.

After a sleepless night, Tess dressed hurriedly and left for the rectory. As she thought, everything was already in motion there. Ladies of the church were bringing in the food for the reception. Dorothy was setting the tiers of the cake together, adding frosting to seal the layers to one another. A punch bowl and cups were set out on a separate table, empty now, of course. They would be filled with a non-alcoholic concoction later. Ice had been purchased from the grocers to keep it cool for the guests.

Tess left the kitchen in Dorothy's capable hands and went to find Meredith still in her room. There was a cool tub of used water and Meredith was sitting in her under things practically catatonic at her dressing table, simply starring at herself in the mirror.

"What does he see in me, Tess? I mean, I am less than average. My one eye is higher than the other and my nose is, well, it never did fit with the rest of my face. My teeth are good but they don't even show when I smile. I don't have cute little dimples or widow's peak. Why, out of all the other women in town, should I get to marry Andrew?" She sounded like a lost child.

Watching Tess in the mirror, she continued, "You know they promoted him. He's manager and will become stationmaster when the railroad extends to town next year along with the telegraph. He will be very important."

Tess moved forward and placed her hands on Meredith's shoulders, bending down so their heads were at the same level. "Where are these doubts coming from? Andrew loves you for being you. He told me he was so glad when you made it clear you liked him. That you wanted him to step out with you. Being shy shouldn't mean you don't get to love the person you were made for. Nothing should stand in your way for true love. The rest of life should fill in the empty space. Never the other way around." Tess saw the doubt in Meredith's eyes.

"Come on, we'll dazzle everyone today with your beauty. Andrew doesn't doubt his love for you. He is probably worried you'll decide you could do better and leave him at the altar," Tess teased her friend. She picked up the brush to fix Meredith's hair into the style, they had decided set the hat off to its best advantage.

The two ladies spoke of less serious things once Meredith's nerves and doubts were put to rest, but Tess, herself, began to think about what she said. Nothing should stand in the way of love. The rest of life should fill-in the gaps not the other way around, no matter how important that other part of life seemed. Tess had started to follow Doctor McLeish's life plan, but her late husband had no other loves in his life except medicine. Tess had the chance of having the biggest love of anyone's life and she had passed it up, put it in second place to pursue a plan she could do anytime.

Meredith stood saying, "Let's try it all on together to see if we were right."

The remark startled Tess into paying more attention to her friend and the special day they were preparing for. Tess would return to her own thoughts later.

The wedding went smoothly and the church was packed. The bride didn't appear as if she doubted her attractiveness or her groom's love and attention. Tess felt so proud to be part of the service. Her heart swelled with emotion.

Tess's contact with Noah was limited once the wedding was over and while the congregation tried to fit into the rectory, flowing out onto the porches since it was a very mild fall day. All the guests made the house overly warm and the men wearing their good Sunday suits took advantage of the cooler air outside.

Tess thought that was where Noah took refuge so she made sure to stay away from those places. She smiled and laughed with the people she knew from town and Sunday service. She was on nodding terms with a few of the relatives from out of town like Meredith's aunt from Austin. Soon the food was mostly eaten and the third punch bowl was half-empty.

A blushing Meredith and Andrew went outside. Tess watched as her friend climbed into the buggy and left with her new husband to spend the next week alone in the house Andrew owned just outside of town.

Dorothy was in charge of cleaning-up so Tess took advantage of the pandemonium of several others leaving the rectory to escape and walk home, letting Buddy out back as soon as she arrived.

Standing in the dark kitchen, Tess gained the full view of the back porch of the house next door as she watched Noah walk up the path. He appeared wary, his gaze roaming over her house as his long strides ate up the distance to his backdoor.

Removing her hat and gloves, she made plans for the evening, gearing herself up for being dismissed if Noah wasn't interested in her any longer. Nothing in his attitude told her he was attracted to her, but then he was very good at hiding his real passions. Tess was hoping he still desired her, she knew desire could be built upon.

Tess called Buddy in and taking a deep breath, walked silently over the grass to step firmly on the porch letting her shoe make enough noise to warn the occupant.

As she pushed open the door, Noah stood at the cupboard and asked, "You want some coffee? I made it with cinnamon."

"I, ah, no, thank you. I ate so much food at the rectory," she told him, not knowing how she was going to proceed if he stayed over in the kitchen.

He didn't. Walking to the couch he sat down, then asked, "You got something on your mind, Doc?"

Tess startled at the endearment and asked, "You back to calling me, Doc, then?"

"It seemed the thing to do since you're over here visiting. You are here to visit, aren't you?" he asked casually sipping at the hot brew.

"I guess so. I was hoping you would like me to, well, to visit you," she answered honestly.

"I can't say I'm not happy. I've had nothing much else on my mind since last night when you were looking at my...at me. I was hoping you remembered what I said when we first met. I had a hell of a time not embarrassing myself for the rest of the evening." He laughed in self-deprecation.

"I didn't mean to make you self-conscious. I let my mind wander and it ended up there. So, I'm here for a friendly visit." She was watching him as she licked her lips unintentionally making his eyes stare at her mouth.

Noah placed the still steaming cup on the table next to him and sat forward, his arms on his knees as he said casually, "I always enjoy a neighborly visit but I need to know this time what the rules are. What are you expecting of me?"

"I'm not expecting anything of you, Noah. I realize I ruined what we had. I was too focused on plans I made years ago. Those took priority over everything we were, everything that should have taken precedence." She tried to explain her behavior the past couple of weeks, but felt she was failing to make him understand how important he was to her. How important his happiness was to her. "I guess finding out I didn't need to put our lives on hold so that I could get my degree made me jump ahead. I went right to what I wanted. I forgot I was no longer alone. It was a very poor choice on my part."

"So, you're here to get an itch scratched?" He hurried on. "Not that I'm against that, of course, just trying to judge the amount of commitment you're expecting."

Tess held her hand out toward him and he accepted it, stood, and followed her into his bedroom.

"How much commitment are you willing to put in?" she asked as she unbuttoned her dress to the waist, pushing it to the floor, then continued to do the same with her lacy camisole.

"As much as you're willing to put in," he answered as he began unbuttoning the top few buttons before pulling the shirt over his head in his urgency to become naked.

They climbed onto the bed, the same lumps in the same places made Tess smile and Noah caught that smile covering it with his mouth, kissing her, silently asking to be allowed in. He sought her tongue and she rewarded him by complying with his need.

His hands molded to her breasts, holding back the needy passion he was afraid would scare her away again. His mouth followed his hands as soon as Tess began making little groans, her hands smoothing and stroking his body, only avoiding the erection that was proudly standing between them. That had been there since his trousers were removed. Who was he kidding?

He had been hard the moment he heard her footstep on the porch.

Noah's hand moved to Tess's hair-covered mound as his mouth descended to her breasts, causing her to arch toward him with her moans coming closer together. He knew she was ready for him and reached over to the drawer next to the bed to retrieve the paper packet, but Tess stayed his hand when he went to tear it open. Noah looked at her in question, fearing she had changed her mind only to find her shaking her head.

"I don't want anything between us again. I want our skins touching as they were meant to, our fluids to mingle as they were meant to, and our bodies to climax and cling to each other as they were always meant to. This is my commitment to you. I love you."

He let the packet drop and covered her mouth with his, letting her know all the desire he ever felt for her was still with them. That he had never been more committed to her, to their being together, than he was at that moment.

"My commitment means I'll marry you come Monday, Tess. No one and nothing will come between us again. I'll work beside you in everything you want to do. I'll never demand anything of you that would take your focus off the clinic or patients. I'll stand by you and do anything you wish as long as you're committed to us when the workday is over. I love you so much."

He spoke while holding himself away from her. He hoped his love and passion showed on his face and the sincerity ran true in his voice.

"I was hoping your commitment would match mine. I agree to everything you've said. I apologize for ever making you think we weren't devoted emotionally to one another. But you are my focus, my life. I love you."

She pulled him to her. He felt his body enter hers, her body respond by clutching him internally, then moving together bringing each other to the pinnacle of ecstatic elation.

She nestled into him, into their embrace where she stayed until the sun was up and Buddy needed to be let out.

EPILOG

Noah showed up as usual near the end of the day with the buggy to pick up his wife from the busy construction site. The little dog yipped happily, tail-wagging, nose in the air sniffing all the interesting smells surrounding the new clinic every day.

"Come on, Doc, that's enough for the day. Mrs. Tyler had dinner almost on and you need to get your feet up or they'll swell like melons," Carter said speaking of their housekeeper and Tess's needs now she was expecting their first child in a few months.

"I'm coming, Noah. I've just been looking through the finished portion of the clinic. Besides, as I keep telling you, walking is good exercise for the baby and me."

She went to climb into the buggy with her husband's help. Noah climbed back onto the bench seat and snapped the reins to have the horse trot back to town. She put her arm through one of his and snuggled into him. Loving being able to call this man her husband, proud to carry his child inside her, anxious to add mother to the list of who she was.

"I know we've discussed this, but I worry about you working so hard. I want to help and feel frustrated thinking my time is almost over. It will be all up to you once the clinic is finished."

"Don't worry, so. I'll be able to get a good three months of surgeries in before your child gets here. Doctor Alexander will arrive in two weeks to train at my side learning my methods. He'll be able to continue the surgical needs until I'm back on my feet after the birth." She reminded her husband calmly. She knew he worried and she knew she could handle the work-load she set for herself. "It's not as if we'll be inundated with patients until we gain a following of local doctors recommending us. I've educated area doctors on diagnosing cancer and the new methods being used to save patients from un-needed pain and death."

"I don't want you giving birth on the operating room's floor so Alexander better know the ropes quickly," Noah said. She knew his edginess was caused by concern. And possibly by hunger.

"We'll have an early night if that would make you feel better about me spending the day out here," Tess placated her overly worried husband.

"Does that mean what I hope it means? You're sure it won't hurt the baby?" He leaned towards her so she could share in his body heat as he wrapped an arm around her.

"Your child is just fine, all cocooned and warm. I won't let anything bad happen to him, Sheriff Carter."

"And I will make sure nothing bad happens to you, Doctor Carter," he replied.

"I depend on that, my love."

She hoped he heard the promise she was making to him again. If not, she would be sure he heard her that night.